# Th

## begins…

As if trapped in a nightmare, Lucy forced herself to peer down into the gaping hole. She was sure she hadn't imagined the sound this time, certain now that it wasn't an animal.

The voice was all too frighteningly human.

"Please!" it was begging her. "Please…"

Pressing both hands to her mouth, Lucy tried not to scream. For she could see now that the grave wasn't empty at all, that there was something lying at the very bottom, camouflaged by layers of mudslide and rising rainwater.

As a sliver of lightning split the clouds, she saw the girl's head strain upward, lips gasping for air. And then the girl's arm, lifting slowly… reaching out to her…

"Please…is someone there…"

Lucy stood paralyzed. She watched in horror as the girl's head fell back again into the mire, as water closed over the anguished face…

# The Unseen

### part 1

## it begins

# RICHIE TANKERSLEY CUSICK

## speak
An Imprint of Penguin Group (USA) Inc.

SPEAK

Published by the Penguin Group

Penguin Group (USA) Inc., 345 Hudson Street, New York, New York 10014, U.S.A.

Penguin Group (Canada), 90 Eglinton Avenue East, Suite 700, Toronto, Ontario, Canada M4P 2Y3
(a division of Pearson Penguin Canada Inc.)

Penguin Books Ltd, 80 Strand, London WC2R 0RL, England

Penguin Ireland, 25 St Stephen's Green, Dublin 2, Ireland
(a division of Penguin Books Ltd)

Penguin Group (Australia), 250 Camberwell Road, Camberwell, Victoria 3124, Australia
(a division of Pearson Australia Group Pty Ltd)

Penguin Books India Pvt Ltd, 11 Community Centre, Panchsheel Park,
New Delhi - 110 017, India

Penguin Group (NZ), Cnr Airborne and Rosedale Roads, Albany,
Auckland 1310, New Zealand (a division of Pearson New Zealand Ltd)

Penguin Books (South Africa) (Pty) Ltd, 24 Sturdee Avenue, Rosebank,
Johannesburg 2196, South Africa

Registered Offices: Penguin Books Ltd, 80 Strand, London WC2R 0RL, England

First published in the UK by Scholastic Ltd, 2003
Published by Speak, an imprint of Penguin Group (USA) Inc., 2005

1 3 5 7 9 10 8 6 4 2

Copyright © Richie Tankersley Cusick, 2003
All rights reserved

LIBRARY OF CONGRESS CATALOGING-IN-PUBLICATION DATA:

Cusick, Richie Tankersley.

It begins / Richie Tankersley Cusick.

p.   cm. – (The unseen ; pt. 1)

First published in the UK by Scholastic Ltd., 2003.

Summary: After a horrifying encounter in a graveyard, Lucy cannot get over feeling that she is
being watched, but is unwilling to trust the one person who might be able to help her.

ISBN 0-14-240463-2 (pbk.)

[ 1. Supernatural—Fiction. 2. Psychic ability—Fiction. 3. Grief—Fiction.
4. Orphans—Fiction. 5. Family problems—Fiction.] I. Title.

PZ7.C9646Itab 2005 [Fic]—dc22 2005043446

Printed in the United States of America

*To Audrey, Suzie, B.J., Lynn, Michele, Victoria and the whole special gang—for your fun, your faith and your friendship. I love you all.*

# Prologue

*She had deceived him!*

He realized now with a terrible certainty that she'd deceived him from the beginning—planned this whole thing from the very start.

And she knew everything about him—*everything!*—what he was and what he'd done and all he was capable of doing . . .

She'd sought him out and gained his trust, for one purpose and one purpose only.

To see him destroyed.

After he'd been so careful . . . so cunning all these years . . . concealing the very nature of his soul . . . the ageless secrets of his kind . . .

And he'd trusted her. Taken her. Loved her more than he'd ever loved anyone.

Tears clouded his vision.

As though he were seeing the future through a dark red haze, a veil of blood.

He glanced down at his hands.

His strong, gentle fingers, wielding the power of life and death.

He hadn't even realized he was gripping the dagger, the dagger of his ancestors, nor did he remember even drawing it from its sheath.

He was gripping the blade so tightly that a stream of his own blood seeped from his fist. He watched it, strangely mesmerized, as it dripped onto the cold stone floor and pooled around his feet.

He hadn't thought he could feel such pain.

Not from the knife, for he had borne far worse injuries than this in his lifetime, had suffered the ravages of a thousand tortures. But those scars had faded quickly, like shadows swallowed by night, and the few that remained were points of honor to him now, sacred testimonies to his very survival.

No, this pain was different.

This pain burned from deep within, filling him with rage and a craving for revenge.

A craving so intense, he could almost taste it.

# 1

She should never have come here.

Not into this deep, dark place, not in this miserable weather . . . and *especially* not at night.

"A graveyard," Lucy murmured. "What was I thinking?"

But that was just it—she *hadn't* been thinking, she hadn't had *time* to think, she'd only felt that sudden surge of fear through her veins, and then she'd started running.

Someone was following her.

Not at first, not when she'd first left the house and started walking, but blocks afterward, six or seven maybe, when the storm had suddenly broken and she'd cut through an alley behind a church and tried to find a shortcut home.

*No, not home!* The words exploded inside her head, angry and defensive. *Aunt Irene's house isn't home, it won't ever be home. I don't have a home anymore.*

The rain was cold. Even with her jacket Lucy felt chilled, and she hunched her shoulders against the downpour, pulled her hood close around her face. She hadn't even realized where she was going; there was no sign posted, no gate to mark the boundaries of this cemetery, just an unexpected gap through the trees. She'd heard the footsteps and she'd panicked, she'd bolted instinctively into the first cover of darkness she could find.

But this was a terrible darkness.

Almost as dark as her own pain.

She crouched down between two headstones, straining her ears through the night. It had taken her several minutes to become aware of those footsteps back there on the sidewalk, and at first she'd thought she was imagining them. She'd thought it was only the rain plopping down, big soft drops, faint at first, but then louder and faster, sharper and clearer. Until suddenly they seemed to be echoing. Until suddenly they seemed to have some awful purpose, and she realized they were coming closer.

She'd stopped beneath a streetlamp, and the footsteps had stopped, too. She'd forced herself to look back, back along the pavement, across the shadowy lawns and thick, tangled hedges, but there hadn't been anyone behind her.

No one she could see, anyway.

But *someone* was there.

Someone . . .

She was sure of it.

And that's when she'd run . . .

"I'm afraid you'll find Pine Ridge very different from what you're used to." How many times had Irene told her that, just in the one agonizing week Lucy had been here? "We're right on the lake, of course, and the university's here, so there's plenty to do. And we're only a half-hour drive to the city. But our neighborhood is quiet . . . rather exclusive, actually. Peaceful and private, just the way residents like it. Not at all like that old apartment of yours in the middle of downtown."

But Lucy had loved her old apartment, the tiny, third-floor walk-up that she and her mother had filled with all their favorite things. And the sorrow she'd felt at leaving it only grew worse with each passing day.

She'd been too depressed on their ride from the airport that day to notice much about Pine Ridge; she had only the vaguest recollections of Aunt Irene pointing things out to her as they'd ridden through town. The college campus with its weathered brick buildings and stately oaks. The renovated historical district with its town square and gazebo; its bars, coffee shops and open-air cafés; its bookstores and art galleries and booths selling local crafts. They'd passed farms and fields to get here, and she'd caught occasional glimpses of the lake through dense, shadowy forests. And there'd been frost sheening the hillsides, and she remembered thinking that she'd never seen so many trees, so many vibrant autumn colors . . .

"And it's safe here in Pine Ridge," her aunt had assured her. "Unpleasant things don't happen."

*You're wrong, Aunt Irene . . .*

Lucy pressed a hand to her temple. That all-too-familiar pain was starting again, throbbing behind her eyes, stabbing through her head, that agony of unshed tears, of inconsolable sorrow . . .

*You're wrong, because unpleasant things* do *happen*—anywhere—horrible, bad things—*and just when you think they couldn't possibly ever happen to* you—

"Oh, Mom," Lucy whispered. "Why'd you have to die?"

For a split second reality threatened to crush her. Closing her eyes, she bent forward and clamped her knees tight against her chest. She willed herself to take deep, even breaths, but the smell of stagnant earth and rotting leaves sent a deep shiver of nausea through her.

*Don't think about that now, you can't think about that now, Mom's gone and you have to get out of here!*

Very slowly she lifted her head. Maybe the footsteps had followed her in here—maybe someone was waiting close by, hiding in the shadows, waiting for her to make the slightest move. Or maybe someone was coming closer and closer this very second, searching methodically behind every tombstone, and she'd never hear the footsteps now, not on the soggy ground, not with the sound of the rain, not until it was too late—

*Come on, move! Run!*

But where? Where could she go? She wasn't even sure where she was, much less which direction to run in.

*"Unpleasant things don't happen . . ."*

Lucy's heart hammered in her chest. She clung desperately to her aunt's words; she ordered herself to *believe* them. Maybe she really *had* imagined those footsteps back there. Maybe it *had* just been the rain and she'd panicked for nothing. After all, she hadn't really been herself since Mom's funeral. As mechanical as a robot and just as hollow inside, moving in slow motion through an endless gray fog of days and nights, confused by the long, empty lapses in her memory. But shock did that to a person, Aunt Irene had informed her, in that cool, detached tone Lucy was beginning to get used to—*shock and grief and the unbearable pain of losing someone you love . . .*

*I can do this . . . . I* have *to do this . . .*

Lucy got to her feet. Steadying herself against one of the headstones, she pushed her long wet hair back from her face, then turned slowly, blue eyes squinting hard into the gloom. High above her the limbs of a giant elm flailed wildly in the wind, sending down a soggy shower of leaves. The sky gushed like a waterfall. As the moon flickered briefly through churning clouds, she saw nothing but graves in every direction.

*Just dead people, Lucy.*

*And dead people can't hurt you.*

The storm clouds shifted, swallowing the moonlight once more. Swearing softly, Lucy ducked her head and ran.

She didn't have a clue where she was going. She'd never had any real talent for directions, and now she ran blindly, stumbling across uneven ground, weaving between headstones, falling over half-buried markers on forgotten graves. She wondered if Aunt Irene or Angela would be missing her about now—or if they even realized she was gone.

"Or care," Lucy muttered to herself.

The truth was, she'd hardly seen Angela since their initial—and totally awkward—

introduction. Angela—with her perfectly flowing waves of jet-black hair and tall, willowy model's figure—had been slumped in the doorway of her walk-in closet, smoking a cigarette and surveying her extensive wardrobe with a petulant frown.

"Angela, for heaven's sake!" Irene had promptly shut off the CD player that was blasting rock music through the room. "This is your cousin Lucy!"

Angela's eyes had barely even glanced in Lucy's direction—huge, dark eyes ringed with even darker layers of mascara. "So?"

It hadn't been said in a rude way, exactly—more apathetic if anything—but Lucy had felt hurt all the same.

"And get rid of that disgusting cigarette," Irene had ordered, shoving an ashtray toward her daughter. "You know how I feel about smoke in the house. And would it kill you to be civil just once? On Lucy's first night here? After all, you two are the same age; you probably have a lot in common."

Angela hadn't flinched. "You're kidding, right?"

"Fine, then. Very fine, Angela. From now on, I don't care *how* the two of you handle it—you girls will have to work things out between yourselves."

A careless shrug. "Whatever."

"Honestly, Angela, you never think about anyone but yourself," Irene had persisted.

Angela had reached over then . . . mashed out her cigarette in the ashtray her mom was still holding. She'd raised her arms above her head, stood on tiptoes, and stretched like a long, lean cat.

And then she'd walked very slowly, very deliberately, out of the room . . .

"Of course they won't care," Lucy muttered again.

She hadn't told either of them she was leaving earlier—she doubted if they'd have understood her desperate need to escape the house where she still felt so lonely and unwelcome. All Lucy had thought about was getting away, and so the darkness of empty streets had felt comforting to her then. But now she felt stupid for being so scared, for getting so lost. She should have gone

11

back the way she'd come; she shouldn't have listened to her overactive imagination.

"Damnit!"

Without warning she stubbed her toe and pitched forward, landing facedown in the mud. For a second she lay there, too surprised to move, then slowly, carefully, she reached forward to push herself up.

Her hands met only air.

Gasping, she lifted her head and stared in horror. Even in this downpour, she could see the deep, rectangular hole yawning below her, and she realized it was an open grave. She was sprawled on the very edge of it, and as she clawed frantically for something to hold on to, she felt the ground melting away beneath her fingers.

With one last effort, she twisted sideways, just as a huge chunk of earth dissolved and slid to the bottom of the chasm.

And that's when she heard the cry.

Soft at first . . . like the low moan of wind through branches . . . or the whimper of a frightened animal . . . faint and muffled . . . drowned by the rush of the rain.

An abandoned cat, maybe? A stray dog? Some poor outcast just as lost as she was, wandering alone out here in the dark? Lucy's heart broke at the thought of it.

"Here, baby!" Stumbling to her feet, she cupped her hands around her mouth and tried to shout over the tremor in her voice. "Come to me! Don't be afraid!"

A rumble of thunder snaked its way through the cemetery.

As Lucy paused to listen, she felt a sudden chill up her spine.

Yes . . . there was the sound again.

Coming from the empty grave.

# 2

As if trapped in a nightmare, Lucy forced herself to peer down into the gaping hole. She was sure she hadn't imagined the sound this time, certain now that it wasn't an animal.

The voice was all too frighteningly human.

*"Please!"* it was begging her. *"Please . . ."*

Pressing both hands to her mouth, Lucy tried not to scream. For she could see now that the grave wasn't empty at all, that there was something lying at the very bottom, camouflaged by layers of mudslide and rising rainwater.

As a sliver of lightning split the clouds, she saw the girl's head strain upward, lips gasping for air. And then the girl's arm, lifting slowly . . . reaching out to her . . .

*"Please . . . is someone there . . ."*

Lucy stood paralyzed. She watched in horror as the girl's head fell back again into the mire, as water closed over the anguished face.

"Oh my God!"

She didn't remember jumping in. From some hazy part of her brain came vague sensations of sliding, of falling, of being buried alive, as the earth crumbled in around her and the ground sucked her down. She lunged for the body beneath the water. She tried to brace herself, but her feet kept slipping in the mud. Dropping to her knees, she managed to raise the girl's head and cradle it in her arms.

"Help!" she screamed. "*Somebody help us!*"

Was the girl dead? Lucy couldn't tell, but the body was limp and heavy and motionless now, the eyes and lips closed. She could hardly see anything in this darkness—only brief flashes of the livid face as lightning flickered over the girl's delicate features. Ghostly white cheeks. Dark swollen bruises. A scarf wound tight around her neck—

"Somebody! *Somebody help us!*"

Yet even as she shouted, Lucy knew no one would hear her. Not through this wind and rain, not in this place of the dead. With numb fingers, she worked feverishly at the scarf, but the wet material was knotted and wouldn't budge. In desperation, she smoothed the girl's matted hair and leaned closer to comfort her.

"Hang on, okay? I'm going to get you out of here, but I have to leave—just for a little while— and get help. I'll be back as quick as I—"

Something clamped onto her wrist.

As Lucy's words choked off, she could see the thin, pale hand clinging to her own . . . the muddy fingers lacing slowly between her own fingertips . . .

They began to squeeze.

"Oh, God," Lucy whimpered, "stop . . ."

Pain shot through the palm of her hand.

Pain like she'd never felt before.

Waves like fire, burning, scalding through every nerve and muscle, throbbing the length of her fingers, pulsing upward through her hand, her wrist, along her arm, piercing her heart and her head. Pain so intense she couldn't even scream. Her body began to shake uncontrollably. Her strength drained in a dizzying rush. Through a blur of strange blue

light she saw the girl's head turn toward her . . .
saw the scarf slip easily from the fragile neck.
She saw the jagged gash across the girl's
throat . . . the raw, stringy flesh . . . the
glimmer of bone . . .

Lucy pitched forward. The girl's body was
soft beneath her, cushioning her fall, and from
some great distance she heard her own voice
crying out at last, though she understood
somehow that this was only in her mind.

"Who did this to you? What's happening?"

*Listen*, the girl whispered. Had her lips
moved? Had she spoken aloud? Lucy didn't
think so, yet she could *hear* this girl, could hear
her just as clearly as two best friends sharing
secrets.

Dazed and weak, she managed to lift herself
onto one elbow. The girl was staring at her now,
wide eyes boring into hers with an intensity
both chilling and compelling. Lucy was helpless
to look away.

*Tell no one*, the girl said, and her lips did *not*
move, and Lucy could only gaze into those huge
dark eyes and listen to the silence. *Do you
understand? Promise me you understand . . .*

Lucy felt herself nod. Tears ran down her cheeks and streamed with the rain over the girl's cold skin. The hand holding hers slid away; the dark eyes shifted from her face, to something far beyond her, something Lucy couldn't see.

*If you want to live*, the girl murmured, *you mustn't tell anyone . . . not anyone . . . what you've seen here tonight.*

"Don't die," Lucy begged. "Please don't die—"

*Promise me.*

"Yes . . . yes . . . I promise."

The girl's eyelids slowly closed.

But for one split second, Lucy could have sworn that she smiled.

# 3

She didn't remember climbing out of the grave.

She didn't remember running or even finding her way out of the cemetery—but suddenly there were lights in the distance and muffled voices and the wild pounding of her own heartbeat in her ears.

Lucy stopped, gasping for breath.

She realized she was standing on a low rise, with a sidewalk about thirty yards below her. She could see streetlights glowing fuzzy through the rain, and beyond that, the watery reflections of headlights from passing cars.

*Oh God, what should I do?*

She couldn't stop shaking. She couldn't get warm, couldn't think. Her knees felt like rubber, and it was all she could do to force herself the rest of the way down the hill.

*Maybe it didn't really happen. Maybe I fell into a hole back there and knocked myself out and started hallucinating.*

She wanted to believe that. Wanted to believe that with every fiber of her being, because to accept what she'd just seen in the cemetery was too horrifying to deal with. Nothing seemed real anymore, not the rain beating down on her or even the nice solid feel of the pavement as she finally reached the curb and peered to the opposite side of the street. There was a gas station on the corner, lights on but pumps deserted, and the voices she'd heard were actually coming from loudspeakers playing country music.

Again Lucy stopped. She glanced behind her into the darkness, into the hidden secrets of the graveyard, and her mind whirled in an agony of indecision.

*I promised. I promised her.*

And yes, it *had* been real, and there was a girl, a girl maybe her own age lying dead, and no matter how sacred a promise, Lucy knew she couldn't just leave her there all alone in the rain . . .

*"If you want to live . . . you won't tell anyone."*

The girl's words echoed back to her, chilling her to the bone. Maybe it wasn't really a warning, she argued to herself, maybe it didn't mean anything at all. She knew people often said strange things when they were dying, when they were out of their heads from pain and confusion and that final slipping-away from the world. *Like Mom was at the end. Like Mom was—*

"No," Lucy whispered to herself. "Not now."

She took a deep breath and shut her eyes, but she couldn't shut out the image of those *other* eyes, those pleading, desperate eyes gazing up at her from the girl's bloodless face. Without even realizing it, she flexed her hand inside her jacket pocket. There was a vague sensation of pain, but she was too preoccupied to give it attention. As she stared over at the gas station, she suddenly noticed a drive-by telephone at one end of the parking area, and she knew what she had to do.

Keeping her head down, Lucy hurried across the street. Someone was working under the hood of a car inside the garage, but the lot was still deserted and the phone was far enough away that she didn't think she'd be noticed. She grabbed up the receiver and punched in 911, telling herself she wasn't *really* breaking her promise. It was only a compromise.

"911. What is your emergency?"

Lucy froze.

*"You won't tell anyone . . ."*

"911. What is your emergency, please?"

*"Promise me . . ."*

"Hello? Please state your emergency."

"Yes," Lucy whispered. "Yes . . . I—"

Without warning a horn blared behind her. Lucy slammed down the receiver and whirled around as a red Corvette screeched to a stop about three feet away. Then one of the windows slid down.

"You picked a hell of a night to run away," Angela greeted her blandly.

Lucy shook her head. Despite the fact that it was Angela, she felt an immense sense of relief. "I'm not running away."

"Oh."

She was sure her cousin sounded disappointed. The thought actually occurred to her to just turn and leave, but then she saw Angela nod toward the passenger door.

"So get in, already. Don't you know enough to come in out of the rain?"

With a last glance at the phone, Lucy hurried around the car and climbed into the front seat. *What am I going to do now?* Anxiously she wiped one sleeve over her wet face, then held out both hands to the heater.

"Look at this mess." Angela rolled her eyes. "You're dripping all over everything."

"Sorry." Scooting back, Lucy angled herself into the corner. She clamped her arms tightly around her chest, but the shivering wouldn't stop. "Do you have a towel or something?"

"No, I haven't got a towel. God, look at my floor."

"I got lost," was all Lucy could think of to say.

Angela grumbled something under her breath. She plucked a lighted cigarette from the ashtray, took a long drag, then blew a thin stream of smoke out through her nose.

"Irene's freaking out," she said at last.

"I'm sorry. I just wanted to take a walk, but then I got all turned around in the storm. I didn't mean to worry anybody—"

"Oh, she's not *worried* about you," Angela

seemed mildly amused. "She's freaking out 'cause you've made her late for a meeting."

Lucy bit hard on her bottom lip. She could feel a lump burning in her throat, anger and tears mixed bitterly together, but she was determined not to cry.

"Well," she managed to whisper. "Of course she would be."

"You should've known better."

"What?"

Angela rolled her eyes. "If you think wandering off like this is gonna get you *any* attention or sympathy from Irene, then forget it. You don't know her."

*But I want to*, Lucy thought miserably, *and I want her to know me, too . . .*

Right after she'd moved here, Lucy had made a habit of studying her aunt's face whenever Irene wasn't watching, longing for just a glimpse of the mother she'd lost. As if somehow her mother's spirit would be reflected in Irene's eyes or in her clothes or in the way she did things—living proof to Lucy that her mom was still with her.

But there'd been no similarities—no similarities whatsoever between the two women—and as the days passed, Lucy only felt more and more abandoned. No matter that Aunt Irene was her only living relative; Irene and Mom were as different as night and day.

Mom had been so . . . well . . . so *alive*. Fun and free-spirited, spontaneous and creative, with the wildest imagination and the most contagious laugh and the most stubborn determination when her mind was made up about something. Lucy had always admired her mother's disregard for rules and routines; there'd always been new things to try and new adventures to share on the spur of the moment. And she'd always loved hearing how much alike the two of them looked—the same blue-gray eyes and long, thick lashes, the same silky blond hair.

Mom had been a source of pride to her. A role model, an ideal she'd always aspired to. She'd never known her father, but Mom had been the best of *both* parents, not to mention her very best friend. Her whole world, really.

But now there was Aunt Irene.

Just Irene, who didn't seem anything like the sister she'd completely shut out of her life. Irene, who barely spoke to Lucy—barely even *looked* at her if she could help it. Who always acted tense and watchful and guarded, as though she expected something bad or dangerous to sneak up on her at any second. Irene and her high-profile job at the university . . . Irene and her endless very important meetings.

"She's self-absorbed," Mom had always told Lucy in those rare moments she ever mentioned Irene's name. "She's always been self-absorbed; she's never thought about anyone but herself. The only thing that makes her happy is getting her own way."

Lucy had never understood the estrangement between her mother and her aunt; Mom had always refused to talk about it. All she knew was that the women hadn't spoken for years, but when Mom was dying, trapped in the last throes of cancer, she'd requested—finally—that Irene be told.

And Irene had come.

To Lucy's shock, Irene had come and stayed—she'd doled out medications, stocked the refrigerator with takeout food, obsessively cleaned and tidied, and remained aloof while Lucy kept constant vigil in Mom's bedroom. And then something had happened one night. Something behind the closed door of Mom's room, something between Mom and Irene alone, something never discussed with Lucy. All Lucy knew was that Mom had suddenly seemed calm and strangely resolved, and the next morning, while Lucy sat beside her holding both her hands, Mom had slipped peacefully away.

Lucy didn't remember much after that.

Over the next few days the funeral had been arranged; over the next few weeks the apartment had been cleared out and rerented, her things had been systematically discarded, packed, or put into storage—all by Aunt Irene, she supposed, for she'd been too numb with grief even to function. And then Irene had brought her here.

"We're your family now, Lucy," Irene had announced in her cool, businesslike way. "This is your home."

And *some home*, Lucy had thought in awe,

laying eyes on the house for the very first time. Compared to the size and comfortable shabbiness of her old apartment, this new place seemed like a mansion, with its white brick walls and tall front columns, its circular driveway, its swimming pool in back. Yet surrounded as it was by thick woods, and only a short walk to the lake, Lucy would have sworn they were in the middle of a vast, lonely wilderness if Irene hadn't assured her that town was only a few blocks away.

Lucy had decided immediately that her life—and her happiness—were over . . .

"Looking for you is *not* how I planned to spend my evening."

With a jolt, Lucy came back to herself. She had no idea how long she'd been buried in her thoughts or how long Angela had been talking. She glanced at her cousin, but those dark-ringed eyes were focused on the rhythmic movement of the windshield wipers.

"I talked her out of calling the police, you know," Angela added.

"The police?" Lucy's tone was grim. "I

thought nothing unpleasant ever happened in Pine Ridge."

"Who told you that?"

"Your mother," Lucy mumbled, wishing they could just leave. She didn't want to sit here any more, here where she could see the cemetery right across the street. She didn't want to sit here knowing what she knew, and she didn't want to remember anything that had happened tonight because she was cold and hungry and exhausted, and if her 911 call *had* been traced, then she *especially* didn't want to be here when the police showed up.

But Angela took another long puff and glanced at Lucy with a tight smile. "How funny."

"What?"

"Nothing unpleasant ever happening here. And Irene—of *all* people—saying so."

Lucy frowned. "What do you—" she began, but Angela cut her off, gesturing vaguely toward the parking lot.

"So what were you doing just now? Trying to call somebody?"

Lucy stole a quick look at the phone box outside the car. How long did someone have to stay on the line for a call to be traced? How long did it take the police to find someone in Pine Ridge?

"Yes." Her mind was racing; the smoke was making her feel claustrophobic. "I was trying to call your house, but . . . but I couldn't remember the number."

"Well, I don't know where you were walking," Angela said matter-of-factly, "but you look like a zombie."

Lucy cringed. She thought of the girl in the grave. A sick taste of guilt welled up inside her, and she swallowed hard, forcing it down. "Can we please go?"

"Oh, great. You're not gonna get sick in my car, are you?"

"I hope not."

To Lucy's relief, Angela instantly buzzed down the driver's window and flicked her half-smoked cigarette out into the rain. Then she rolled the window up again, sat back, and turned up the heater full blast.

"Thanks," Lucy said. "I appreciate it."

"I didn't do it for you. I did it for my car."

*Of course you did. What was I thinking?* Lucy

tensed, listening. Was that a siren she'd just heard in the distance? Or only a muted sound from the radio? *Please . . . please . . . let's just leave . . .*

"Look, let's get this straight. If you came here expecting money, Irene's not gonna change her will. You're not gonna get one bit of the inheritance." Angela's voice was stony. "Just so you know."

Lucy faced her in surprise. "I didn't come here for your money. I didn't come here for anything, Angela. I didn't even *want* to come here—it wasn't *my* idea. Your mother *made* me come here." She hesitated, then said, "Just so *you* know."

"She's not my mother," Angela muttered.

"What?"

"I said, she's not my mother. She's my stepmother." Reaching over, Angela readjusted the heater again, then leaned back with an exasperated sigh. "My father married her when I was ten. And then he died two years later, and I was *stuck* with her. We've *never* gotten along, Irene and me—we've *always* hated each other. And I'm *leaving* here just as soon as—"

Abruptly Angela broke off. She reached for a

31

fresh cigarette, and Lucy could see how she trembled with anger.

"As soon as I turn eighteen," Angela finished defiantly. She held a lighter to the tip of her cigarette, the tiny spark glowing orange in the dark. "As soon as I'm eighteen, I'm taking off for New Orleans," she murmured again. "That's when I inherit my money, and I can do what I want. Till then I'm a goddamn hostage."

Lucy gave a distracted nod. *No . . . no . . . it's not a siren. It's going away now, in another direction . . .*

Taking a deep breath, she tried to focus once more on the girl beside her.

"I didn't know anything about you," Lucy admitted, unsure what else to say. "Not about you *or* Irene. My mom barely mentioned Irene the whole time I was growing up. I'm really sorry."

Angela's eyes widened, almost mockingly. "Sorry? Don't be sorry for me. Don't *ever* be sorry for me—I can take care of myself just fine."

"Angela, I didn't mean—"

"Just forget it. Who the hell do you think you are?"

*I don't know anymore*, Lucy thought miserably. *I used to know, but everything's different now . . . I'm different now . . .*

She was beginning to feel sick again. She wanted to leave, wanted Angela to stop talking and start driving. She could feel the girl's eyes upon her, and she could still see the eyes of that dead girl, and there was too *much* death, death in her past, and death tonight, she was drowning in it, drowning in all this death, and *if we don't leave right this minute I'm going to totally lose it and start screaming—*

"God, what'd you touch?" Angela asked suddenly.

"Touch?" A chill crawled up Lucy's spine, though she managed to keep her voice steady. "What do you mean?"

And Angela was leaning closer now, staring harder, her eyes like big black hollows in the shadows of the car.

"There," Angela told her. "There on your hand."

Startled, Lucy looked down.

She stared at the narrow black welts on the back of her right hand and between her fingers, at the misshapen black stain on the skin of her palm. In one more quicksilver flash, she saw the girl in the open grave, remembered the girl's hand closing around her own . . .

"I . . . I don't know," she heard herself whisper. "When I fell, maybe. That's what happened . . . I tripped . . . and I must have bruised myself when I fell."

For an endless moment there was silence.

"That's no bruise," Angela said at last.

She pulled the Corvette back onto the street and peeled away, but Lucy scarcely noticed.

Because the thing on her hand really *didn't* look like a bruise.

It looked like a burn.

Like something had burned itself right into her skin.

# 4

He'd come back one last time.

Just to make sure she was dead.

Some killers didn't like to come back, he realized, for fear of being seen, being connected in some way, being caught—these dangers, of course, were of no concern to him.

But after he'd done what he had to do, he couldn't get her out of his mind. He'd stood at his window watching the rain, replaying her voice over and over again in his head—her pleas for mercy, her screams of pain. And suddenly he'd begun to grow restless. Restless in a way he couldn't understand, a strange uneasiness in his veins that made him pace in the dark and jump at small sounds and warily watch the shadows.

And so he'd come back.

One last time.

She was just as he'd left her, naturally, and this soothed him a little. He'd stood over the crumbling grave and he'd stared down at her, and he'd stood for such a long, long time, waiting to see if she'd speak, if she'd move, if her eyes would open, if she'd look at him in the old familiar way he'd so loved being looked at.

But she didn't move.

And she didn't say his name.

The water and the mud were over her face, from the walls of the grave caving in, and if he hadn't put her there himself, he'd never have known she was there at all, he'd have thought she was just a pathetic mound of soggy earth at the bottom of the yawning hole.

He really was so amazingly clever.

The old graveyard. A violent storm. No one in Pine Ridge would even consider venturing into this place tonight.

So he'd thrown his arms wide to the rain, and his hair had blown wild in the wind, and he'd sucked in the darkness, until it filled him and sated him and consumed him and—

And then that restlessness again.

That vague, creeping uneasiness, gnawing in the pit of his soul.

He'd actually felt a moment of doubt.

And so he'd lowered himself into her grave.

He'd knelt down beside her and wiped the mud from her face, and he'd studied her in death, all the while wondering about her final moments of life.

She would have lingered awhile. Been aware of the warm blood pumping from her throat, leaking out between the torn chunks of her flesh, spurting with every heartbeat, then growing weaker . . . weaker . . . until it became merely a thin trickle, melting into the soggy earth.

The thought made him smile.

She was no threat to him now.

She was dead, and he was free.

And so he'd leaned over, oh so gently, and he'd put his mouth upon hers . . . cold lips together . . .

And then he'd kissed her.

One last time.

# 5

God, it was freezing in here.

*It must be me*, Lucy thought, as she slid lower in the claw-footed tub, closing her eyes, trying to relax beneath the bubbles. The bathroom was large and luxurious just like the rest of the house, but even with central heating, and even with the water as hot as she could stand it, she couldn't seem to get warm.

*What am I going to do?*

She could smell takeout pizza wafting up from the kitchen, and her stomach gave a queasy lurch. She could hear the muffled sound of the TV downstairs, and Angela's rock music blaring from the next room. And though Aunt Irene was now en route to yet another very important meeting, Lucy could still picture that formidable frown waiting for them when she and Angela had gotten home. Lucy had been relieved when Irene ordered her straight upstairs and into a hot bath. She hadn't felt like explaining any more details about her evening.

*So what am I going to do?*

She felt drained and bone-tired. Like her whole body had gone comatose and her brain had fizzled out. The cemetery . . . the girl . . . the warning . . . everything seemed like a distant dream now, or something she'd seen in a horror movie. An out-of-body experience that had happened to someone else's body . . .

"Hey!" Angela banged on the door. "Don't use up all the hot water!"

It was almost too much effort to answer. Groaning, Lucy roused herself and called back, "I'm not."

"And don't go to sleep and die in my bathtub."

"I wouldn't dream of it."

"Dinner's ready."

"I'm not hungry."

"Don't you like pizza?"

"Not three nights in a row."

Gently she massaged her forehead. She could imagine Angela leaning against the other side of the door, filing her fingernails and admiring the shape of her hands. No wonder her cousin looked practically anorexic, she thought— there hadn't been a single healthy or home-cooked meal in this kitchen since Lucy had been here.

The music abruptly shut off.

"If you die in there, you'll bloat and be all wrinkled," Angela informed her.

Lucy sighed. She listened to Angela's footsteps fading down the stairs, then she closed her eyes and drifted lower into the water.

*I have to do something.*

*I have to tell somebody.*

She couldn't call from here, that was certain. She didn't have a cell phone, and it would be too risky trying to call the police from a phone inside the house—too easy to be traced.

But besides that, something else was bothering her.

And even though she'd forced herself not to think about the obvious truth of the matter, she couldn't avoid it any longer. It had been lurking there in the farthest reaches of her mind, a mocking shadow keeping just beyond consciousness, ever since she'd made her gruesome discovery.

But now she had to face it.

*Someone killed that poor girl.*

Someone had *murdered* that girl, and not mercifully.

The death wound hadn't been clean or swift; someone had hacked at her throat, leaving her alone and helpless and frightened, leaving her to bleed to death in the rain.

Which meant the murderer was still out there.

*And if I tell, he might find out.*

*And if he finds out it was me, then he'll kill me, too.*

Trembling, Lucy readjusted the loose coils of hair she'd pinned on top of her head. She wrung out her washcloth, molded it to her face, and eased farther down into the water, resting her head against the back of the tub.

*Could he have seen me? Could he have followed me?*

Again she thought back, trying to convince herself she was safe: it had been so dark, storming so hard, she'd had the hood of her jacket pulled down around her face. And if the murderer really *had* been close by, wouldn't he have stopped her *then*? Done whatever he had to do to keep her from leaving?

No, something told Lucy that she and the girl had been the only ones out there in the cemetery. At least for those brief, terrifying moments.

Still . . .

A gust of wind rattled the bathroom window. Lucy jerked the washcloth from her face and sat up straight, her heart pounding.

*At least you were with her at the end . . . at least she wasn't alone . . .*

As the overhead light flickered, Lucy grabbed for her towel on the rack. Holding her breath, she waited. Within several minutes the lights slowly regained brightness, so she dried off quickly, pulled on her nightgown, and hurried through the connecting door into her bedroom.

*Not my bedroom,* she reminded herself grimly. *My prison.*

For the first two days after she'd come here, she'd simply stayed in bed, sleeping and crying, then sleeping again, missing her mother so much that her soul felt raw. The containers of takeout food that Irene regularly left on her dresser went virtually untouched. She hated the stark white walls and carpeting. She hated the sleek white furniture that looked like something straight out of a decorating magazine. She'd been so depressed, she hadn't even bothered to put out any of her favorite personal things. What she'd brought with her was still packed in boxes and suitcases, stored upstairs in the attic, all of them painful reminders of her happy life that had died.

"I'm sure you'll love your room, Lucy," Irene had assured her on the plane ride here. But Lucy had hated it at first sight, hated everything about it, including the sheer-curtained sliding doors that opened side by side out onto a little wrought-iron balcony, making her feel both exposed and accessible. She even hated the giant mulberry tree that grew beside it, the one that scraped and clawed at the railing and eaves and made it sound as though someone were trying to break in and kill her every single night.

*God, Mom, what were you thinking, sending me here?*

Sighing, Lucy shut off the overhead light and left just the lamp burning on the nightstand by her bed. She could hear Angela slamming cupboard doors in the kitchen and then tromping back up the staircase.

Lucy gritted her teeth and counted to five.

Angela's CD player blasted through the upstairs, vibrating the floors, rattling the windowpanes. Ten ear-shattering seconds of rage and defiance—Lucy knew it was ten, for she'd clocked it many times—before the volume cut off and silence reigned again, everywhere but in Angela's headphones.

*It's a miracle she hasn't gone deaf by now,* Lucy thought glumly. Rubbing her ears, she walked over and stood in front of the sliding doors.

Her room was at the back of the house, separated from Angela's by their adjoining bathroom, and at the opposite end of the hallway from Aunt Irene. From here she could look down onto the manicured lawn; the brick patio and terraced wooden deck; the glassed-in hot tub; the swimming pool, covered now for the winter; the landscaped flower beds and mulched pathways and discreetly camouflaged woodpile, all coated with a thin layer of frost. At the rear of the lawn stood a low stone wall with a gate, and beyond that, a narrow pathway led through dense woods to a private stretch of lake. Despite the heavy rain, a pale gray fog had begun to ooze through the trees. Lucy watched it, strangely fascinated, as it wound its way toward the house, smooth and silent as a snake. There was no moonlight. Only an occasional burst of lightning managed to rip the storm clouds and illuminate the landscape below.

Shivering, Lucy started to turn away.

And then she saw something.

*What* is *that?*

Frowning, she leaned closer, squinting hard through the glass.

Had she imagined it? That very slight movement just beyond the wall? As though one shadow had separated itself from all the others . . . as though it were hovering there, like a wisp of pale smoke, just on the other side of the gate . . .

*Come on, Lucy, get a grip.*

Of *course* there were shadows out there—*millions* of shadows out there—and of *course* things were moving. *Fog and wind and rain and—*

"Some animal," Lucy whispered. *A deer,*

*probably.* She'd spotted an occasional deer in the yard since she'd been here. Irene hated them, said they caused major damage to her expensive shrubs; she'd forbidden Angela to leave out food of any kind.

"Just a deer," Lucy told herself again, more firmly this time.

And yet . . .

Frowning, she pressed closer to the doors, lamplight soft behind her. *"Peaceful and private"* —isn't that what Irene had said about this neighborhood? Yet Lucy could feel a vague sense of unease prickling up her spine. As though something far more ominous than a deer was out there in the woods . . . watching her.

*Don't be ridiculous . . . it's because of what happened tonight . . . you're only imagining things.*

She thought of the girl. Of her own promise. She wondered again what she should do. She didn't want to stand here looking out anymore, but she couldn't seem to turn away from the dark.

Her breath quickened. She could feel her heart fluttering in her chest. Only moments ago she'd been freezing, but now a peculiar warmth was spreading through her, hot liquid in her veins. Her favorite nightgown, much too thin for these unforeseen autumn nights, now seemed unusually constricting. She opened the first three buttons down the front and leaned forward, resting her forehead against the glass.

Something moved on the corner of her balcony.

Gasping, Lucy's head came up, and she peered anxiously out into the night. *Just the tree . . . that stupid tree hitting the railing . . . nothing more!* But even as she tried to reason with herself, she was already tugging at the doors, sliding them open to the wind.

Rain swept savagely into the room. With a cry, Lucy grabbed both doors and after a brief struggle, managed to lock them in place. Then she backed away and sat on the edge of her bed, soaking wet.

*What on earth were you thinking?*

She was cold again—cold to the bone—and besides that, she felt unbelievably stupid.

"And paranoid," she reminded herself glumly. "Don't forget paranoid."

As her mind flashed back to the cemetery, she tried to block it out. No wonder she was seeing watchers in the woods now, and lurkers on the balcony, and danger in every shadow. And thank God Angela was buried in her headphones right now, completely oblivious to the rest of the world—Lucy wasn't up for any more confrontations or excuses.

Leaving her gown in the bathroom to dry, Lucy toweled off and changed into a warm pair of sweats. Then she shut off the lamp and tried to cocoon herself deep inside her blankets.

She lay there, wide-eyed, too exhausted to sleep.

She lay there feeling numb, and each time a vision of the dead girl floated into her mind, she tried to think of other things. *Home before. Mom before. My perfect and wonderful life before.* She'd had friends . . . she'd been popular . . . she'd had fun, and she'd had ambitions. What were her friends doing now, she wondered sadly. She'd withdrawn from them more and more during Mom's illness, and since she'd come here to live, she'd scarcely thought about them at all—hadn't written, hadn't even called. She'd promised a few of them to keep in touch, to send them her address—why hadn't she?

*Because I hate it here so much. Because I'm so miserable, and I don't want them to know how horrible my life is now . . .*

Her thoughts swirled and faded. The storm continued to rage outside her windows, and after a very long time she finally drifted off.

She wasn't sure what woke her.

It was a feeling rather than a sound.

A slow, cold chilling at the back of her neck . . . a vague sense that she wasn't quite alone.

Lucy struggled to open her eyes. She was lying on her side facing the sliding glass doors, and as lightning flashed beyond the rain-streaked panes, the room went in and out of shadow.

"Lucy," a voice said softly.

Raising herself on one elbow, Lucy stared. She could see the curtains blowing in, billowing like lacy feathers, though she knew it was *impossible*, that she'd already shut those doors, already bolted them tight against the wind—

"Lucy . . ."

Her eyes widened in alarm. A sob caught in her throat.

"Mom?"

She tried to struggle up in bed, strained her eyes to see. And yes, the curtains *were* moving, fanning out like delicate wings, only there was something *else* there, too—a hazy figure silhouetted against the glass—she could *see* it now, though it was flimsy and formless, as sheer as those fine gauzy curtains . . .

"*Mom!*" Tears streamed down Lucy's cheeks. "Mom, is that you?"

"Listen to me, sweetheart."

And it *was* her mother's voice, but so sad, so sad. *Why does she sound like that, so terribly sad and hopeless . . .*

"Mom—"

"Be careful, Lucy," the voice whispered, and it was already fading, scarcely more than a breath. "You're going to a place where I can't help you . . ."

"What do you mean, Mom? No, *wait!* Don't leave! *Please* don't leave me!"

Lucy flung out her arms, reaching . . . reaching . . .

But the mournful shadow was gone now . . .

And the curtains hung pale and soft and deathly still.

# 6

A knock.

Two loud knocks, and then another, firm and persistent, hammering their way into her warm, cozy dream.

"Go away," Lucy mumbled.

She was decorating the Christmas tree in their apartment. Mom was baking gingerbread men for all her fourth-grade students, and they were both singing carols at the top of their lungs, and Mrs. Manetti from downstairs was bringing up homemade soup later for all of them to share . . .

"Wake up, Lucy. You'll be late."

"Go away," Lucy said again, only this time the dream faded down a dark tunnel, and her eyes opened to hazy light and someone standing in the open doorway to the hall.

"We've already discussed this," Irene said firmly. "I said I'd give you one week to settle in. Today you're going to school."

"Today?" She was wide awake now, the announcement finally sinking in, along with a feeling of panic. "But it's Friday—why can't I wait till next week?"

"Because one day will be difficult enough to get through. And you'll have the entire weekend to recover before you start fresh on Monday."

"But it's too soon! I'm not ready!"

"You can ride with Angela, so hurry up."

Irene didn't wait for a response, and this time Lucy didn't give one. She lay there with her face buried in the pillow, too stunned to move. Her eyes felt swollen, as though she'd been crying . . . her whole body felt achy and stiff. She wondered if maybe she was catching the flu, yet there was a vague sense of uneasiness nagging far back in her mind.

*No, not the flu. Something else . . .*

Something dark and suffocating . . . something gnawing at the distant edges of her mind . . . something bad that she couldn't quite place . . .

*Something horrible. But what?*

Groaning softly, she turned onto her side. Her right hand was aching, as though she might have wrenched it in her sleep, so she propped herself on one elbow and leaned over to examine her palm.

Memory slammed her full force.

As every horror of last night came back to her in shocking, grisly detail, Lucy let out a cry and felt the room spin around her. How could she have forgotten—even for a moment! *The girl— the grave—my promise—*

She'd hoped so much to be wrong. That somehow she'd only imagined it in her mind, that it had only been a nightmare, that she'd wake up this morning and realize the whole thing had never happened!

But it *had* happened.

And now, as Lucy stared down at her hand, she could see the evidence all too clearly, the truth etched deeply into her skin.

It was a strange marking.

Not at all as it had looked last night, for the ugly welts and discolorations had practically faded away. Now there was only the smallest reminder—the pale, puckered flesh of a tiny scar—stamped into the exact center of her right palm. It looked like a sliver of something. Like a sliver of moon. *That's it . . . a crescent moon.* So perfectly formed, it seemed neither random nor accidental. As if some miniature branding iron had been used to sear a pattern into her flesh.

*No. No, that's crazy.*

Grabbing the blanket, Lucy rubbed it vigorously against her palm. These were crazy thoughts she was having, thoughts that didn't make sense, because this scar on her hand was just that—a *scar*—a *wound*—nothing more. She'd tried to help, and in their struggle the poor girl had scratched her, and eventually this little scar would fade, too . . .

*But how did it heal so fast?*

Lucy let go of the blanket. Despite the fact that she'd been rubbing so hard, her scar wasn't even red. She stared at it in disbelief, remembering how gruesome her hand had looked last night, remembering the excruciating pain she'd felt when the girl had grabbed her in the cemetery.

*What's happening to me? Am I having some kind of nervous breakdown?*

"Lucy!"

Angela's voice shocked her back to attention. The door from the bathroom flew open, and Lucy saw her cousin scowling at her from the threshold.

"What am I, your private chauffeur?" Angela's miniskirt barely covered her crotch. Her designer sweater looked as if she'd spray-painted it over her chest. She looked like an expensive hooker. "You're not even up yet, and I am *so* not waiting for you."

"Yes," Lucy nodded, throwing off the covers. "Yes, I'm hurrying."

The door slammed shut. As Lucy sat up in bed, she tried to ignore the sick feeling in the pit of her stomach. When had she eaten last—sometime yesterday? So much had happened since then . . . so much confusion in her head. She couldn't think straight. She couldn't think at all.

She closed her eyes, then opened them. Her gaze traveled slowly around the room. She could see the windows . . . the sliding doors . . . the slow dawn of an autumn morning struggling to break through.

*Mom . . . I saw Mom . . .*

Lucy's heart caught in her chest. *Yes . . . Mom was here . . . she said something to me . . .*

Her mind tried frantically to remember. She could almost hear the tone of her mother's voice . . . could almost see her mother's face . . . but the words she'd spoken were completely gone.

Frustrated, Lucy got up. She padded barefoot to the sliding doors and squinted down at the carpet, as if she expected to see a footprint or a distinctive clue, some confirmation of her mother's visit. She ran a tentative hand down the length of the curtains, and her eyes misted with tears.

*Of course she wasn't really here. It was just a dream. She wasn't here, and she wasn't a ghost either, because ghosts don't exist . . .*

Lucy opened the curtains and peered out. A watery sun was spreading across the backyard, and she could see Angela recklessly scooping seeds into all the bird feeders. The rain had stopped, but beneath a cold November sky lay the widespread destruction from last night's storm—piles of wet leaves, splintered tree branches, strewn garbage, uprooted plants, even a few wood shingles and a broken shutter—and as Lucy's gaze shifted to the stone wall in back, she saw that the gate was standing open.

Her heart clenched in her chest. She forced herself to take a deep breath.

*It doesn't mean anything. It was just the storm.*

"Just the storm," Lucy repeated to herself. Of *course* nobody would have been out there watching her window in the middle of a storm—she'd just been feeling overly paranoid last night. As fierce as the wind had been, it was a miracle the gate was even still there at all.

She let the curtains fall back into place.

"*Lucy!*" Irene shouted.

"Coming!" Lucy shouted back.

She hurried to the bathroom, but couldn't resist checking the clothes hamper first. There were her clothes, right where she'd tossed them last night, totally covered in mud. *What did you expect—isn't that scar proof enough for you? Are you still hoping last night didn't happen?* She picked up her toothbrush, squeezed toothpaste across the bristles. *Think, Lucy, think!* Why was it so hard to focus this morning? Why couldn't she brush her teeth without trembling? *Maybe I can sneak out of school and find another pay phone . . . maybe I can pretend I have an emergency and borrow someone's cell phone—cell phones can't be traced, can they?*

Lucy frowned at herself in the bathroom mirror.

*I'll have to go back to the cemetery on my own. I'll have to go back there and find her. It's the only thing I can do.*

Yet she knew in her heart it was pointless. She was certain the girl was dead—*had* been dead now, for nearly twelve hours. Not only that, but she'd been lost last night, panicky and disoriented—she didn't have a *clue* where the cemetery was. *And even if you* do *manage to find the cemetery, even if you* do *manage to find the grave—what then?*

What if the killer had come back, what if the killer were *there*? What if he really *did* recognize her from last night—she'd be as good as dead.

Sighing, Lucy leaned closer to her reflection. She had dark bruises under her eyes, and her normally tan complexion was pale. She'd never worn much makeup—Mom had always insisted that Lucy had a natural sort of beauty—but today she added a touch of blush and lipstick. Just for color, she told herself. *Just for confidence, you mean.*

"Angela's right," she sighed. "I *do* look like a zombie."

She didn't even know what outfit to put on—what did kids in Pine Ridge wear, anyway? She wasn't prepared for the chilly autumn weather here, and she'd never needed warm clothes at home—no matter what she picked out this morning, she was sure to look stupid. She made a face at the mirror and tied her hair back in a ponytail. Then she went to her room, took jeans and a pale blue sweater from her dresser drawer, and pulled on thick socks and sneakers.

"Lucy! Angela is waiting!"

"I'm coming!"

God, this was going to be an awful day. As if everything else weren't bad enough already, just thinking of going into a new school, and being introduced and having everyone stare at her, made her feel sicker than ever.

She could hear the TV as she came downstairs. Pausing on the bottom step, Lucy listened nervously to a brief review of the local news. Nothing about a murder. No body discovered anywhere. Not knowing whether to feel relieved or not, she started into the kitchen when the sound of voices stopped her just outside the door.

"You can't do this to me!" Angela cried angrily. "It's not fair!"

Then Aunt Irene, cold and utterly calm. "I told you if you got one more speeding ticket, you'd be grounded. You had plenty of warning."

"But the Festival's this weekend!"

"Keep your voice down. You're acting so high-strung—are you coming down with something?"

"Yes. Dreams. I'm coming down with dreams, Irene. Weird, sexy ones, all night long. Send me to the hospital."

"Angela, will you please be mature this morning? Must we go through this—"

"Every single day?" Angela finished. "I *have* to go to the Festival. *Everyone's* going! I *have* to be there!"

"You should have thought of that before. And you should have known better than to think I wouldn't find out about this latest ticket."

"Oh, right, I forgot. Your personal friends on the police force. Or was it the judge this time?"

"This discussion is over. You can use your car to drive to and from school, but nowhere else. There will be no social events of any kind until I say so."

"It's not even about me, is it?" Despite Angela's sarcasm, Lucy could hear the threat of tears. "It's just about you looking bad in front of your important friends—"

"That's quite enough, Angela."

"If it was Lucy, you wouldn't ground *her*."

"If it was *Lucy*, I wouldn't be *having* these problems."

"Right." Angela's tone was suddenly as cold as her mother's. "Right, I forgot. 'Cause Lucy's so goddamn perfect."

Lucy pressed a hand to her mouth. She heard the kitchen door fly open.

"Angela, come back here," Irene ordered. "You have to take Lucy to school."

"*You* take her," Angela threw back. "It was *your* idea to bring her here—*you* take her!"

The door slammed shut with a bang. As tears sprang to her eyes, Lucy flattened herself against the wall and fought down her own wave of anger. *Thanks a lot, Irene. Do you think you can get Angela to hate me just a little bit more?*

"Lucy!" Irene fairly shrieked.

Quickly Lucy went back to the stairs, then came noisily down the hall again, as though she'd just arrived.

"Yes, here I am. Sorry."

"Get in the car. We're already late."

"I thought you said Angela—"

"I forgot she had some errands to run before school. I'll be taking you. Where's your jacket?"

"I . . . it got so wet last night, I—"

"Here. Take this jacket of Angela's. She'll never miss it."

"But—"

"Just put it on, Lucy. I can promise you she will *never* wear it, simply because *I* gave it to her. And Angela would rather *die* than be seen in *anything* I pick out for her. I'm sure it will fit you nicely."

63

"If you say so."

Irene was silent for the whole drive. It wasn't until they pulled up in front of the high school that she finally graced Lucy with a comment.

"I know classes have already started this morning, but as you know, I've spoken with Principal Howser several times. He's assured me that everything's been taken care of, so all you need to do is go straight to his office. He'll be expecting you."

"Thanks. I'll be fine."

"I'm sure you will be. Have a nice day, Lucy."

As her aunt drove off, Lucy stood there on the pavement and made a quick assessment of the school: two-story buildings of ivy-covered brick; stone benches placed strategically around the wide, sweeping campus; a covered courtyard with tables and chairs; an outdoor stage; rows of bleachers and an athletic field in the distance. Lots of trees, lots of windows, lots of cars in the parking spaces, *lots of students to face . . .*

Taking a deep breath, Lucy took one hesitant step toward the gate. Then she stopped.

*You don't have to do this now. You can wait and go Monday. You can tell Irene you got sick and had to go home, and it's not really a lie, and it's not like one more day will make that much difference . . .*

Lucy turned slowly, her eyes scanning the sidewalk and street beyond. A quiet, residential area; nothing but houses as far as she could see. But she'd noticed a post office and a grocery store on their drive here—someone was sure to know where the cemetery was.

She glanced over her shoulder at Pine Ridge High.

Then she ducked her head and hurried away from the school.

# 7

It didn't take long to find what she wanted.

But then, standing beneath the weathered sign of PINE RIDGE CEMETERY, she realized it didn't look anything like she remembered.

There hadn't been gates where she'd come in before; there hadn't been a fence or a sign. *Maybe this isn't the right cemetery, maybe Pine Ridge has more than one.* But the old man she'd asked outside the post office hadn't even hesitated— he'd pointed her straight in this direction. The old part and the new part, he'd explained to her, with the empty old church still standing guard at one end. *You were disoriented last night, you were terrified, of course nothing's going to look the same today.*

Lucy glanced up and down the narrow, deserted street. Directly across from her was an empty lot; a block away, the street suddenly ended, giving way to an overgrown field and a rickety, boarded-up house set far back beneath some trees. There was no traffic here. Not a single pedestrian in sight.

*Well, what are you waiting for? Just go in and get it over with.*

Lucy began walking. She hadn't expected the place to be so big—much bigger than it looked from the sidewalk—with row upon row of perfectly aligned headstones and carefully placed markers. The grass was spongy, littered with remnants of last night's storm. Plastic flowers lay everywhere, along with shredded plants and broken vases, toppled wreaths and even some soggy toys.

As Lucy walked farther, she began to notice a distinct difference in her surroundings. How the ground seemed to be actually sinking, rainwater standing in shallow pools . . . how the trees seemed to be pressing closer, weaving their branches more tightly overhead. And *yes*, she thought suddenly, fear and hope beating together, fluttering in her chest—*yes, this all seems familiar . . .*

Back here, so far from the cemetery's entrance, these graves had been forgotten. Patches of dead weeds pushed against tombstones; piles of dead leaves obliterated names. It was colder here, and piercingly damp. Locks hung rusted from mausoleum doors, heavily shrouded in spiderwebs. Stone angels and sleeping children, once meant to be comforting, now gazed back at Lucy with hollow eyes and moldy faces, their tender smiles rotted away. As though weary of their burden, many headstones had slipped quietly beneath the ivy; others were crumbled to dust.

Lucy stopped beside an unmarked grave and lowered her face into her hands.

*What am I doing here, Mom? Can you even believe this?*

Suddenly she was furious with herself. She must have been insane to come here, wandering around alone in this isolated place instead of being in school! *Did you really think you'd find her—some dead girl in an open grave?* There were *hundreds* of burial plots in here—*thousands*, probably!—how long could she possibly keep searching? Not to mention how enraged Irene would be when she found out Lucy had skipped school.

"Bad idea," Lucy whispered to herself. "*Very bad idea.*"

Forget good intentions—she'd leave this place now and find a pay phone. Promise or no promise, she'd make an anonymous call to the police, and then she'd get back to the house. She'd go straight to bed, and when Irene came home, she'd swear she really *had* been sick all day, but next Monday she'd be—*miraculously!*—recovered and more than ready to begin her new life.

Resolved, Lucy raised her head. She hunched her shoulders against the cold, dank breeze and turned back the way she'd come.

She was scarcely aware of his shadow.

There were so many of them, really, surrounding her in deep, dark pools . . . soft and black like liquid, oozing between the graves, seeping beneath the low-sweeping branches of the trees . . .

And later she would wonder how he got there—appearing without a word or a sound— just suddenly *there*, his tall shadow figure blocking her path, one arm extended in front of her to prevent her escape.

She saw him gazing down at her—eyes without light, face without features—or was it her own fear distorting his image, blurring everything into an indistinct mask? She wanted to run, but she was frozen in place; she heard his voice, but it seemed like some strange, faraway echo.

"She's not here," he said. "The one you're looking for."

Lucy could barely choke out a whisper. "What? What are you talking about?"

And the angels were watching—all around her, Lucy could see their blank, empty stares . . . their dead, decaying eyes . . .

The stranger was above her now.

Leaning over . . . reaching out . . . a sharp black silhouette against pale, pale light.

"She's not here," the stranger said again. "He's taken her away."

# 8

Someone had ahold of her shoulders.

As Lucy fell back a step, she realized that strong hands were trying to steady her, to keep her facing forward. She willed herself to scream, but all that came out was a frightened whimper.

"Take it easy," a voice said. "Just breathe."

*Breathe?* Struck by a fresh wave of panic, Lucy began to struggle. The hands holding her immediately tightened their grip, and before she realized what was happening, she felt herself being pulled tight against her captor's chest.

"Stop it! I'm not going to hurt you."

Lucy stopped. With her arms pinned securely to her sides, she looked up to see a pair of dark eyes gazing back at her with calm, cool intensity. In a split-second appraisal, she guessed him to be a little over six feet tall, with a strong, lean build, probably about her own age, possibly a year or two older. High cheekbones accentuated the angles of his face; a faint shadow of beard ran along his chin and jawline and upper lip. His hair was thick and as black as his eyes, falling in loose, tousled waves to his shoulders. And he held himself very straight—though not so much a formal posture, she sensed, as a wary and watchful one.

Lucy realized she was staring. As fear and confusion coursed through her, her mind scrambled for some self-defense tactic, but the rest of her still felt too stunned to cooperate.

"I'm not going to hurt you," he said again. "I just want to talk."

He released her so unexpectedly that she nearly fell over. Recovering herself as best she could, Lucy watched as he took three steps back, then he raised his hands into the air where she could see them.

"You ran away," he stated. His eyes narrowed slightly, yet the piercing stare never wavered, even when Lucy began to back up.

"What do you mean?" she demanded. "I don't know what you're talking about. Who are you?"

Her heart was racing like a trip-hammer, her thoughts spinning in all directions. *He knows about the girl—how could he know? The only way he could possibly know anything is if he was* here—*if he was the one who—*

"You tried to help her, but it was too late. And if you tell anyone—anyone at all—you could die." His tone was so even, so matter of fact—which somehow made it all the more frightening.

Lucy's voice rose. "You don't know *anything*! You don't know—"

"And they wouldn't believe you anyway—"

"*Who are you?*"

"I'm Byron. I want to help you."

"I don't know you! And I don't need your help! Why are you doing this? Why are you saying these things?"

"Because they're true."

Slowly he lowered his arms. He slid his hands into the pockets of his jacket, and he turned his eyes to the ground, and when he spoke, Lucy could hear the cold contempt in his voice.

"It's not your fault, you know. You couldn't have saved her. Nobody could."

Tears blurred Lucy's vision. Wheeling around, she was finally able to run.

*This is insane! This can't be happening!*

She realized she was crying, crying so hard she couldn't see, and her chest was hurting, and her lungs were aching from the cold. She slid on wet leaves and sank ankle-deep in mud. Every breath she took was a knife blade between her ribs.

God, why had she ever come here this morning? How could she be so stupid, what could she possibly have been thinking?

And now, on top of everything else, here was some psycho lurking in the graveyard, acting like he *knew* her, acting like he knew about what had *happened* here last night—*some psycho who must be the murderer, who else could he be?—he saw me and he knows who I am and now it's a game—cat and mouse—he's taunting me and now he's going to kill me, too—*

"You're in danger," the voice warned.

Lucy screamed. She hadn't heard him following, hadn't seen him coming, but now

74

her back was flat against a tree, and he was *standing* there, just inches away, gazing at her with those dark, dark eyes.

"People know I'm here!" she babbled. "They'll be looking for me—they'll be worried if—"

"I told you, you don't have to be afraid of me. I'm a friend."

"Leave me alone! I don't have any friends!"

"But you need one. Someone you love is gone now . . . you need one."

Lucy gaped at him. A wave of nausea rose up from her stomach, lodged in the middle of her throat. *I'm going to be sick . . . Oh God, I'm—*

"Sorry about your mother," he whispered.

As Lucy drew an incredulous breath, all feelings of nausea vanished. She simply stood there with her mouth open, staring at him in utter disbelief.

"Someone told you." At last her words choked out, tight with fury. "Someone *had* to tell you! My aunt or—or—my cousin—or someone at school—"

"No one had to tell me. I see it in your eyes."

She was vaguely aware of a rushing in her

head—a churning mixture of shock and rage and despair—and the tears that wouldn't stop, still pouring down her cheeks. For a moment she couldn't think, didn't even realize that she'd moved toward him, or that her hands had clenched into fists or that she'd shoved them hard against his chest.

"You really expect me to *believe* that?" she cried.

She saw him shake his head. Saw his hands close firmly over her fists, though he made no move to push her away.

"Some things take time to believe in," he said solemnly. "And right now . . . we don't have a lot of time."

As Lucy stared at him in bewilderment, he eased her hands from the front of his jacket. Then, still holding her wrists, he leaned down toward her, his voice low and urgent.

"Something happened here last night. Something important."

*Yes,* she thought desperately, *a murder. A cold-blooded murder and—*

"I think something touched you."

"You don't know anything," Lucy whispered.

But *"What'd you touch?" Angela had asked . . . and the dying girl's hand, squeezing so hard . . . the pain, the horrible pain, the excruciating pain . . . and "That's no bruise," Angela had said . . . That's no bruise . . .*

"I think something was . . . passed on to you," Byron murmured.

Lucy's eyes widened. As she tried to pull free, Byron's grip tightened, forcing her closer. With one smooth movement, he turned both her hands palms-up and gazed down at the tiny, crescent-shaped scar.

"Let go!"

Jerking from his grasp, Lucy stumbled back out of reach. She could feel her right hand beginning to tingle—ice-hot needle pricks spreading out from the center, out to her fingertips—and she clamped it shut and thrust it deep into her pocket. She told herself it was just the cold, told herself Byron had just held her too tight, shut off her circulation, but her hand was stinging . . . feeling so strange . . . and it was starting to tremble, just like her knees were trembling, just like her voice was trembling . . .

"Stay away from me!" she burst out. "I don't know why you're here, and I don't have a *clue* what you're talking about, and I'm *not* afraid of you!"

For a long moment Byron stared at her. "It's not me you need to be afraid of," he said at last.

It took every ounce of courage to turn her back on him. Holding her head high, Lucy made her way determinedly back through the graves, and she told herself that she wouldn't look back.

But when she did, he was still standing there, and she couldn't help thinking how very much he resembled some dark angel, some ominous messenger in the midst of all that death . . .

"Be careful," he called to her then, his voice as heavy as the shadows around him. "Someone won't be glad you're here."

# 9

The whole morning had been a disaster.

*A complete, miserable, and utter disaster.*

Lucy stood in the doorway of the cafeteria, clutching her books to her chest. She let her eyes wander over the laughing, chattering mass of students, then turned and walked slowly down the hall. She hadn't planned on coming to school this morning after her visit to the graveyard; she'd wanted to find a way back to the house and hide there and try to make sense of things—until she suddenly remembered she didn't even have a key.

She hadn't tried to find a pay phone. *"You tried to help her . . . it was too late . . ."* She hadn't reported last night's murder. *"You can't tell anyone . . . you could die . . . they wouldn't believe you anyway . . ."* She'd been so frightened, so thoroughly shaken by her encounter with Byron, that she didn't even realize she'd retraced her steps back to school. She'd simply looked up and found herself standing outside Pine Ridge High, wondering how she'd gotten there.

*Oh, God. What's happening to my life?*

She'd stared at the school, and she'd weighed her options—*Could I spend the day hiding out in some coffee shop? The library? How about the bus depot?*—but she hadn't been able to come to a single decision.

*He* knew *things! Byron* knew *things about last night, he knew things about* me *he couldn't possibly know!*

She'd rested her head against the fence while the world passed in a blur. He was a total stranger, but he'd known about her mother. He was a total stranger, yet it was almost as if he'd been *waiting* for her there, as if he'd *expected* her to show up there this morning . . .

Maybe he really *was* the murderer, Lucy thought again. And maybe he really *had* been taunting her, playing with her, trying to see how much she really knew. *So why didn't he kill me? Why didn't he kill me right then, when he had the perfect chance?*

She hadn't been able to shut out his words: *"She's not here . . . the one you're looking for . . . he took her away . . ."*

His words . . . those frightening, fateful words playing over and over and over again, relentlessly through her brain—

*"We don't have a lot of time . . ."*

*"Be careful . . ."*

*"Someone won't be glad you're here."*

She'd stood outside Pine Ridge High, afraid to go in, afraid to go anywhere, until a teacher hurrying into the building had spotted her and ushered her to Principal Howser's office. To Lucy's relief, the man had actually believed her story about being sick that morning. He'd welcomed her warmly and offered deep condolences for her loss; he'd praised her high grades from her former school, and he'd talked about how wonderful Aunt Irene was. He'd gone on and on about some Festival the school was having, and how he hoped she'd enjoy living in Pine Ridge. Then he'd handed her a schedule, assigned her a locker, given her a tour, and escorted her to class.

"Here we are, Lucy. I believe your cousin Angela has Miss Calloway this hour, too."

*Wonderful. My morning's complete.*

He'd interrupted a pop history quiz to introduce her, leaving her to stand like an idiot at the front of the room while Miss Calloway tried not to look annoyed and all the kids had stared. She'd felt flushed and panicky and embarrassed. Some of the kids were laughing, she'd noticed—some of the girls whispering to each other, some of the guys whistling loudly. And then she'd spotted Angela, sitting in the very back row, snickering loudest of all.

It wasn't till she'd run to the bathroom afterward that Lucy realized she had dead leaves stuck in her hair and mud spattered over her clothes. She'd stared at her sorry reflection in the mirror and felt so mortified, she'd actually considered hiding in there the rest of the day.

*Wonderful, Lucy, just wonderful. Leave it to you to make a great first impression.*

But at least the humiliation had distracted her.

At least it had kept her from dwelling on the cemetery . . . the murdered girl . . . *Byron* . . .

Thank God lunch was over now; she had only a few more hours to get through.

By the time Lucy found her next class, her head was pounding. Dull ribbons of pain crept down one side of her face and unfurled behind her eyes. She was achy and stiff, her shoes and socks were damp, and she still hadn't had anything to eat. Her mind was worn out from worrying; her brain had turned to mush. She didn't have a clue how she was going to make it through math. Like a robot, she slid into her assigned desk and saw Angela sitting right beside her. The dark raccoon eyes fixed on her accusingly.

"I've been thinking about that jacket of yours," Angela frowned, leaning toward her.

Lucy braced herself. "What about it?"

"It looks really familiar to me. In fact, I have one exactly like it."

"I know." Lucy kept her gaze lowered. "Irene said I could borrow it."

"And you didn't even *ask* me?"

"You were already gone. And she said you never wear it anyway, because she gave it to you."

"I can't *believe* this!" Angela pulled back as several kids squeezed between them, book bags swinging dangerously. "*Look* at it! It's totally *ruined!*"

Someone bumped Lucy's desk and murmured an apology. She glanced up to see the back of his faded jacket as he leaned over the desk in front of hers. Then Angela snapped her back to attention.

"Did you hear what I said?"

"I heard you," Lucy sighed. "I'll pay to have it cleaned, okay?"

"You'll pay to buy me another one, is what you mean. God, who do you think you are?"

To Lucy's relief, Mrs. Lowenthal called the class to order and instructed them to take out their books. Then, while the woman droned on and on about numbers that made no sense, Lucy tried to ignore the venomous looks Angela kept shooting at her from across the aisle. *Don't let her get to you . . . right now Angela's the least of your worries . . .*

"—announcements regarding the Fall Festival," Mrs. Lowenthal was saying. Fall Festival? When had they finished with math? When had they stopped working problems on

84

the chalkboard? Lucy didn't know . . . hadn't been paying attention.

Something soft hit her foot. Glancing down, she saw what looked like a necklace lying there on the floor, but she had no idea where it had come from. Her eyes did a quick sweep of the class, but everyone was focused on the front of the room. Lucy scooted the necklace closer with the toe of her shoe, then picked it up to examine it.

It was a simple piece of jewelry—nothing expensive, elaborate, or even professional, she thought. Just a single strand of tiny beads, dark green glass, that looked rather childishly handmade. *Pretty, though, in a plain sort of way . . .*

"—want all of you there early if you're working a booth," Mrs. Lowenthal continued.

Lucy put her left hand to her forehead. Was it just her, or was the room getting hotter by the second?

"—big fund-raiser of the year, as you all know," Mrs. Lowenthal said.

It *was* getting hotter in here, Lucy was sure of it. She could feel drops of sweat along her hairline; she shifted uncomfortably in her chair.

"—those volunteers will meet this afternoon in the library—"

*Maybe I'm coming down with something—getting a fever—God, I'm burning up—*

"—be sure to check the schedule to see which shifts you're working—"

Lucy slid lower in her desk. Her head was way past throbbing now—it felt like it was going to burst. She wound the necklace around her wrist, twined it between her fingers; she could feel the tiny beads cutting into the tender flesh of her palm—

"—can use my car to transport some of the food—"

For a brief second the room shimmered around her. A tingling pain shot through her hand, and Lucy tried to brace herself against the desktop, tried to prop herself up, but her wrists were so limp, so useless . . .

*What's happening?*

She couldn't hold her head up anymore. She couldn't hear . . . couldn't see—yet at the same time she could see *everything*, *hear* everything, everything all at once, every single sense wide open—

*What's . . . happening?*

The classroom vanished. The warmth building steadily inside her now burst into scalding heat, searing through nerves and muscles, throbbing the length of her fingers and upward through her hand, along her arm, exploding inside her head.

*I've felt this before—oh God—just like last night—*

And then they came.

Lightning fast and just as merciless—images so vivid, so sharp, her body reeled with the force of them—

*Hands—such powerful hands—eyes glowing through shadows—lips on her neck, her throat, and blood flowing, life flowing, "Could have been different . . . could have been perfect . . ."*

*Wind! Ah, the cold, sweet rush of it, taste of it, caress of it—night smells night sounds damp and cold! And fog so thick . . . woods so black . . . black and deep as—*

"Death," Lucy murmured. "I'm not afraid to die . . ."

*And "Lucy?" . . . someone saying her name, over and over again, "Lucy . . . Lucy . . ."*

"Lucy?" Mrs. Lowenthal's voice, anxious and loud. "Lucy, are you all right?"

Lucy's eyes flew open.

She was slumped on her desk, both arms pillowing her head. She was clutching something in her right hand, and her whole arm felt numb and prickly, as if she'd been shot full of novocaine.

"Lucy?" Mrs. Lowenthal said again.

Very slowly Lucy lifted her head. She could see that the classroom was there again, along with the faces of the students, all of them staring, and Angela smirking beside her, and Mrs. Lowenthal leaning over her with a worried frown.

"You're so pale, Lucy, are you ill? Do you need to be excused?"

Lucy tried to answer, but couldn't. Instead she opened her fingers and stared down at the necklace in her hand.

"I'll have someone take you to the nurse," Mrs. Lowenthal decided. "Angela can help you. Here, Angela, let me write you a pass."

But Lucy wasn't paying attention anymore to Mrs. Lowenthal or Angela or the curious stares of her classmates.

As the guy in front of her turned around, she saw that he'd taken off his jacket. She saw the thick black hair falling soft to his shoulders, and the calm gaze of his midnight eyes. And then she saw him reach back and slide the necklace from her hand.

"Thanks," Byron said quietly. "I must have dropped this."

# 10

She knew she was going to be sick.

As Byron faced forward again, Lucy got to her feet and rushed up the aisle to the door. Then, ignoring an alarmed Mrs. Lowenthal, she hurried down the hall in search of a bathroom.

She finally found one near the stairs, barely making it inside before dry heaves took over. She left the stall door open and fell to her knees, sweat pouring down her face, her insides like jelly. She dreaded Mrs. Lowenthal coming to check on her—or even worse, sending Angela.

"This might help," a voice said softly.

Lucy was too weak to lift her head. She felt a cold, wet paper towel on the back of her neck . . . a gentle hand smoothing her hair back from each side of her face.

She heaved again, but there was nothing in her stomach but pain.

"Thank you," she managed to whisper.

"No need," the voice whispered back to her. "The first time's always the worst."

Lucy lifted her head.

Turning around, she stared out at the bare floor, at the row of sinks and the dingy mirror stretching over them, reflecting nothing.

"Hello?" she called shakily. "Who's there?"

Her voice echoed back to her from the bathroom walls. With trembling fingers, she took the paper towel from the back of her neck and got slowly to her feet. One by one, she moved down the row of stalls and opened each door, but they were all empty.

"*The first time's always the worst . . .*"

Without warning a group of girls came giggling in from the hallway. Was one of them the kind-hearted stranger? But none of the girls even glanced her way, so Lucy ran fresh water onto the paper towel and blotted it over her face. Mrs. Lowenthal was right—she *was* pale— *frighteningly* pale. *Think, Lucy, think! Try and calm down . . . try to put things in perspective . . .*

Perspective? How could she possibly be calm or rational about all the things that had happened to her in the last twenty-four hours? She was way past confusion now—way beyond frightened. Something had taken hold of her back there in the classroom—something had *consumed* her back there in the classroom— something she didn't understand and certainly hadn't been able to control. Something had crept over her and through her, transporting her to another place and time—she'd *seen* things, *felt* things—*horrible* things, intense and painful and terrifyingly real, and yet . . .

And yet there'd been no *complete* picture, Lucy realized. Nothing like a carefully posed photograph or neatly framed painting or smooth sequence of movie scenes running logically through her mind.

No, this had been different.

Just flashes of things, glimpses of things, puzzle pieces spilled helter-skelter from a box. Things without order, things that made no sense, though she felt they *should make sense*, and *did* make sense somehow, if only she could put them together . . .

Frowning, she stared down at her hand. The strange crescent scar stood out sharply against her palm, and there was a faint, lingering ache along her fingertips.

*The necklace.*

Lucy shut her eyes . . . opened them again . . . drew a slow intake of breath.

*There was darkness . . . and death . . . and it started when I picked up that necklace . . .*

The bathroom door swung shut. As Lucy turned in surprise, she realized that all the girls had left, and that Angela was now standing beside her.

"I've been looking all over for you." Angela gave an exasperated sigh. "What the hell happened back there?"

Lucy couldn't answer. She watched dully as her cousin leaned toward the mirror and primped at her hair.

"Well?" Angela demanded.

"I . . . felt like I was going to pass out," Lucy murmured.

"I've never seen anyone shake like that before they passed out," Angela said, casting Lucy a critical glance. "God, you look even worse now than you did last night. Whatever you've got, you better not be contagious."

"Who's the guy in class?" Lucy asked tersely.

"*What* are you talking about?"

"The dark-haired guy sitting in front of me."

"Byron?"

Lucy nodded, tight-lipped.

"Well, what about him?" Tilting her head, Angela gave her hair one more fluff. "Oh, please. Don't tell me you're *interested*."

Lucy merely shrugged.

"Right. Another smitten female falls under the spell of the mysterious Byron Wetherly," Angela announced. Then her lips curled in a dry smile. "Well, yeah, he's gorgeous. *And* sexy. *And* so very, *very* cool. But . . . you know . . . every girl in school is after him."

She paused a moment, as if considering a matter of great importance. Then she lifted one eyebrow, amused.

"Frankly, Lucy, I wouldn't bet on your chances."

Ignoring the remark, Lucy pulled a fresh paper towel from the dispenser. "What do you mean, mysterious? Why is he mysterious?"

"Well, who knows *anything* about him, really? He keeps pretty much to himself."

"Maybe he's shy."

"He doesn't talk much. But with a face and body like that . . . why would he need to?"

"I see." Lucy played along. "The quiet, secretive type. *That's* what makes him mysterious."

"Not just that. His family, too."

"So his *family's* mysterious."

"They're poor." Tilting her head sideways, Angela studied her profile in the glass. "And extremely weird. I mean, the word is that Byron must be adopted or something—he's the only normal one in the whole bunch. He lives with his grandmother—well, takes *care* of his grandmother; she's an invalid. His mother's been locked up for years."

Lucy looked startled. "Locked up?"

"As in *loony bin*? As in *institution*?" Angela pointed to the side of her head and made wide circles with her finger. "As in *psychopathic maniac*?"

"Yes, Angela, I get it. What's wrong with her?"

"She murdered her kids."

"Come on . . . you're not serious."

"Burned down the house with them in it. Oh, for God's sake, it happened years ago. I'm not sure anyone around here even remembers the woman *personally*—it's just something everyone knows about." Angela paused, thought for a second, then once again faced the mirror. "You know. Like a campfire story. Or one of those urban legends."

"But what about Byron?" Lucy asked.

"Well, *obviously* he got out, didn't he? Him and his crazy sister. Are you finished in here?"

Lucy nodded. She ran some water over the towel, squeezed it out, then pressed it against her cheeks, stalling for a little more time.

"So . . . is the mom in prison?" she asked.

Angela rolled her eyes. "No, just in a straightjacket for the rest of her life. Poor Byron. I mean, can you even imagine? Everyone knowing your mother's a cold-blooded killer? And, like *that's* not bad enough, that sister of his was turning out just as bad—it was only a matter of time before *she* got carted off to the funny farm. Lucky for everybody, she ended up leaving town before anything really horrible happened."

"I guess that *was* lucky," Lucy agreed quietly. "So tell me about the sister."

"She *saw* things." Another dramatic sigh. "Well . . . at least that's what she wanted people to believe. She *saw* things."

"You mean . . . like hallucinations?"

"Call them whatever you want—*she* called them *visions*."

Lucy's heart caught in her chest. She was feeling colder by the second. "What kinds of visions?"

"How would *I* know? *I* never saw her have one." Angela sounded impatient. "Telling-the-future-and-talking-to-the-dead kinds of visions, I guess. I mean, the girl was *way* creepy."

"So she never had a vision in school?" Lucy's voice was scarcely a whisper.

"She didn't go to school. She didn't go anywhere, really. I mean, nobody ever saw her."

"Then if nobody ever saw her . . . how do you know she even existed?"

Angela gave a sniff of disdain. "Well . . . nobody *normal* ever saw her. Nobody *I* know ever saw her. But there were stories, you know?" Leaning closer to her reflection, she rubbed at a tiny smudge of lipstick on her tooth. "Sometimes people would drive past the Wetherly place at night, and they'd see her watching from an upstairs window with bars on it. And sometimes, people just going down that road at night would hear screams coming from inside the house. That's why they never let her out. She was totally dangerous."

Despite her uneasiness, Lucy frowned. "Sounds like old wives' tales to me."

"Whatever. But she ran away last year, so that was a big relief to everybody. *Especially* to Byron, I imagine. I mean, God, how humiliating—so *not* cool for his social life. Now there's only him and his grandmother." She paused, her brow creasing in thought. "Good thing he's so gorgeous—he certainly doesn't have good breeding going for him."

"Then how can you really know him?" Lucy asked tightly. "How can you be so sure he's *not* like his mother? *Or* his sister?" *How can you be sure he doesn't stalk unsuspecting victims, or murder girls in cemeteries, or see into a person's mind . . .*

"Well . . ." Angela's look was blank. "That's just silly."

"*Why* is it silly? You said he keeps to himself . . . that no one really knows him—"

"God, what is this whole *obsessing* thing?"

"What about his life away from school? What about his private thoughts? What about his feelings?"

Angela made no effort to hide her amusement. "His feelings? Oh, I'd like to feel him, all right—in places *besides* my fantasies. Just like every other female around here."

She stepped back from the mirror. She ran a slow gaze over Lucy, then shook her head in mock disappointment.

"Poor Lucy . . . take my advice, okay? Forget about Byron. As a matter of fact, forget about *anybody*. You look like you've been run over by a bus. And you just had some kind of weird fit—not to mention nearly throwing up—in the middle of class. I mean, it's so *embarrassing*. Everyone already thinks you're a freak, and it's only your first day."

It took all Lucy's effort to compose herself. She wadded up her paper towel, tossed it into the trash, and carefully smoothed the front of her sweater. "You know what? I'm actually feeling much better. In fact, I don't think I even need to see the nurse now."

"Then why'd I waste my time trying to find you?"

Biting back a reply, Lucy followed Angela back to class. Byron didn't even glance at her as she slid into her seat, didn't seem to feel her eyes boring into him as she tried to ignore the stares and whispers around her. He was out of his chair as soon as the bell rang, and though Lucy hurried to catch up with him, he'd already disappeared into the crowded hallway by the time she reached the door.

She didn't see him again the rest of the afternoon, neither in class nor on campus. As though he'd vanished from her life just as quickly as he'd appeared.

By the time the final bell rang, Lucy was never so glad to have a day end—it took every last effort just to drag herself to her locker. Everywhere she turned, there was talk about the big weekend ahead, exciting plans for the Fall Festival, but all *she* planned on doing was locking herself in her room and staying in bed. She was just rechecking her homework assignments when Angela showed up, greeting her with a sullen frown.

"Hurry up," Angela complained. "I have better things to do than stand around and wait for you all day."

"You just got here. You've been waiting for—what? Two whole seconds?"

"Do you want a ride or not?"

Lucy slammed her locker door. Lowering her head, she did a quick assessment of her books, oblivious to the kids shoving past her till she felt a quick, light pressure on her arm.

"What?" Startled, she looked up. Angela was standing several feet away, watching her with growing impatience.

"What?" Angela echoed.

"Did you just touch me?" Yet even as she asked, Lucy knew it hadn't been Angela. Somehow, in that precise moment, she *knew* it was the girl who'd come to her aid in the bathroom. *That's impossible . . . how could I know that?*

"What are you talking about?" Angela frowned.

Immediately Lucy stood on tiptoes, anxiously

scanning the corridor. It was packed with students eager to start the weekend, but none of them seemed to be paying any attention to her.

*This is just crazy.*

"Someone touched my arm," Lucy insisted. Puzzled, she turned to Angela, who was now making an exaggerated show of checking her watch.

"You *think*?" Angela threw back at her. "I mean, there're only about a *million* people around here bumping into each other."

"No, but . . ."

"But what?"

"This was different. It wasn't an accident. She . . ."

"She, who? She, *what*?"

*She wanted me to know.* The realization came to Lucy with warm, calm clarity. *She did it on purpose because she wanted me to know she was here, that she was* real, *that I* didn't *imagine her—*

"You're not gonna have another fit, are you?" Angela was regarding her warily. "Because if you are, I'm leaving."

"No," Lucy murmured, taking one last

puzzled look around. "No . . . I'm ready."

"Then let's go."

For once, Lucy didn't mind Angela's music blaring—in fact, she hardly even noticed it at all. While her cousin sang loudly off-key all the way home, Lucy leaned her head against the window and tried to sort out all the troubling events of the day. *Explanations? None. Logic? None. Worry factor? Definitely rising. And Byron . . .*

She could still see those dark, dark eyes searching hers . . . hear the edge in that low, deep voice . . . feel those strong hands on her shoulders. It was his ominous warning that had finally convinced her *not* to report the dead girl . . . at least not yet. She'd been frightened of him, still *was* frightened of him—only now that fear was tempered with an almost fascinated curiosity. He had answers—she was sure of it—but answers to things she *wasn't* sure she wanted to pursue. As the car pulled into the driveway, Lucy wished she could ask her cousin more about Byron—but she didn't dare. Her life was complicated enough already without having Angela any more involved.

The house was empty when they went in. As

Lucy shut herself in her room, she thought she heard Angela scrolling through the messages on the answering machine . . . thought there might be one from Irene, though she couldn't make it out. She stood for a moment with her back against the door, eyes closed, weary relief flooding through her body.

And then her eyes opened with a start.

*What's that smell?*

A very faint fragrance . . . and pleasantly sweet . . . yet nothing she recognized, nothing she could recall ever having smelled before . . .

Frowning, Lucy dropped her stuff on the desk and walked to the sliding glass doors. She opened them all the way, letting in crisp fall air, then she stepped out onto the balcony and stared off across the lengthening shadows over the lawn.

The woods still looked menacing, even in the last few hours of daylight. A slight breeze was blowing, and as Lucy gazed into the trees' shifting patterns of darkness and fading autumn colors, a shiver crept slowly up her spine.

*That feeling again . . .*

*That feeling of being watched . . .*

"Bad habit," Lucy muttered. "Get over it, for crying out loud."

Irritated with herself, she turned back into the room.

She took a few steps, then stopped abruptly by the bed.

*That's strange . . .*

Despite the fresh air blowing in, she could still smell that aroma . . . delicate . . . sweet . . . and . . . *something else . . .*

Lucy tilted her head. Breathed deeply and long.

The fragrance flowed down easy . . . soft and smooth as wine . . . velvet in her veins . . .

*Intoxicating.*

*Yes . . . that's it. Intoxicating.*

Light-headed, Lucy reached out a hand toward her bed. She sat down unsteadily, then lay back and closed her eyes.

The scent floated from the covers.

Like an exotic perfume, it rose up around her, enveloped her from every side—sheets, blankets, pillows, comforter—even her nightclothes, which she'd carelessly tossed across the headboard that morning in her hurry to dress. It seeped into the pores of her skin, and brushed softly across her eyelids, and tingled along the fingertips of her right hand . . .

And that's when Lucy realized.

That's when it hit her full force that someone had been in here today.

In her room . . .

And in her bed.

# 11

"Lucy! What the hell are you doing?"

Lucy could hear Angela shouting at her from the bathroom doorway, but she didn't care. She didn't care, and she didn't stop—she kept right on stripping the linens from her bed.

"Lucy! Did you hear me? You know we have a cleaning lady who does that!"

"I don't care about the cleaning lady—I don't want to *wait* for the cleaning lady. I want these off now. I want them washed. I want clean sheets. I want a new bedspread. I want—"

"Have you totally lost your mind?" Angela yelled. "Florence was here *today*! Everything already *is* clean!"

Lucy froze. She stood there like a statue, then very slowly turned around.

"Today?" she murmured. "You mean . . . the cleaning lady—"

"Florence, yes, our cleaning lady. She always comes on Fridays—"

"That's not true. My room's different. Someone was in my room."

"You've hardly come *out* of your room since the first day you got here," Angela reminded her sharply. "Irene told Florence not to go in there till you felt better. So today she cleaned it."

*No . . . that's not right.*

Lucy stared at her cousin with a puzzled frown. Of course it made perfect sense . . . of course it must be true . . .

"There's . . . a smell," she finished lamely.

Angela came farther into the room and sniffed.

"Well, *yeah*—probably air freshener. Or furniture polish. Or stuff she puts in the carpet. Florence always sprays *everything* around here. *Especially* when we've been sick or something."

*No! That's not right!*

"You are so weird." Angela glowered at her. "Didn't anybody ever use air freshener where you came from?"

Lucy didn't answer. She sank down on to the foot of the bed and gazed in bewilderment at the sheets and blankets piled around her on the floor.

"Put on something warm," Angela said then. "We're going to the Festival."

"What?" Lucy looked up just in time to see her cousin disappear into the bathroom. "We're doing . . . what?"

"Going to the Festival!" Angela's voice hollered back to her. "It's Friday night—I can't stand to be here one more second!"

"But you're not supposed—" Lucy began, then stopped. Not a good idea to let Angela know she'd eavesdropped this morning, that she'd heard Irene grounding the girl. But not a good idea either, aiding and abetting a criminal . . .

*Your choice. Get out or stay in this creepy room.*

She heard the shower running, so she went over and shut the door. Then she crossed her arms over her chest and leaned back against the wall, studying her bed as though it were some unwelcome alien dropped in her midst.

*I don't believe you, Angela. Why don't I believe you?*

Lucy was beginning to think Angela might be right—that maybe she truly *was* losing her mind. Some sweet-smelling air spray had sent her into a complete tailspin—she'd jumped to the most ridiculous conclusion. Someone in her room? Well, of *course* someone had been in her room—*Florence* had been in her room, simply doing her job!

And yet . . .

Lucy chewed mercilessly on a fingernail. Something inside her—*deep* inside her—still felt uneasy . . . uneasy and unconvinced. *Why?* She'd always been so sensible, so logical, always prided herself on her levelheadedness. But that was before the cemetery, she reminded herself now. Before the girl in the grave . . . before all the *other* crazy things that had happened to her, *before I started jumping at every shadow and letting my imagination spin entirely out of control—*

"Florence," Lucy said firmly to herself. "Florence, Florence, Florence. Florence the cleaning lady."

But, *no*, her mind answered her, without the slightest hesitation . . . *No, not Florence . . .*

*Someone else.*

"Lucy!"

Startled, Lucy looked up to see Angela glaring at her from the doorway again.

"Irene has a very important meeting tonight that'll last till at least eleven. If we leave now, we can beat her home."

Lucy couldn't resist. "And why would we want to do that?"

"I've been having some car trouble." Angela didn't miss a beat. "I promised her I wouldn't be out on those dirt roads after dark. Just, you know, in case something should happen."

"I see."

"So if we're back early, she won't have to know about it. I mean, I wouldn't want her to worry."

Lucy shook her head. "Of course not."

"So come on!"

The door slammed between them, and Lucy gazed at it for a few seconds, wrestling with her conscience. It *would* be better than staying here in this room right now. And since she wasn't supposed to know Angela was grounded, *she* certainly wouldn't be the one in trouble if Irene discovered they'd gone out. Besides, Lucy reasoned, doing this for Angela might help make a truce between them.

It was just the Fall Festival, after all.

And what could possibly happen to them at a Festival?

# 12

He'd been fascinated when he'd first seen her—
that beautiful girl at the window.

He hadn't been able to turn away, gazing at
her through the trees, through the rain—he
hadn't expected anyone to be there, hadn't
even realized there was a house at the edge of
the woods. Once his work was done at
the graveyard, he'd needed a safer, darker
sanctuary, and so instinct had driven him deep
into the moonless shelter of the forest.

He often prowled after he'd killed.

City streets . . . neighborhoods . . . country
roads . . . any convenient place to work off those
lingering effects of restlessness and release.

He hunted unhindered. Undetected.
*Unseen* . . .

It amused him to stand over people while

they slept . . . people who didn't know he was there, people unaware that their lives were in his power. With one quick decision he could determine if they awakened tomorrow, or if they languished for hours or days on end, or if their hearts stopped suddenly, midbeat, without the slightest warning.

Just as *his* heart had had no warning when he saw her there at the window.

He'd watched her curiously, the light glowing pale behind her, the outline of her soft, sweet curves beneath the flimsy fabric of her nightdress. At one point he thought she might have seen him, too, for she was peering at the woods, at the low stone wall . . . but he was always much quicker than a glance. He'd been a shadow for a while, and then a wisp of fog. He'd watched her unbuttoning her gown, the delicate swell of her breasts as she'd leaned forward against the glass, and then he'd been outside on her balcony as she'd slid open the doors and gotten drenched from the rain. He'd reached out and touched her cheek, but she hadn't known; he could have gone inside with her, but he'd waited.

He didn't need an invitation—not from her,

not from anyone—he went where he pleased, when he pleased.

*How* he pleased.

But her sorrow had stopped him.

Like a fragile aura, it surrounded her and flowed from her—he could feel the palpable grief, the vulnerability and despair, and though it would have been so easy, so pleasurable, to take her then, he'd decided against it.

He'd taken the other girl instead.

The other girl had left her window open just the tiniest crack, and he'd slipped through the screen, slipped right inside on the cold, wet breeze, and he'd stayed till nearly dawn. Even in slumber she'd reeked of anger and rebellion, and he'd found this exciting, this wild, defiant nature so very much like his own.

She'd thought she was dreaming, of course.

When he'd pulled down her covers without the slightest disturbance . . . when he'd caressed her naked body with his eyes, his hands, his mind . . .

Her thighs had parted, her back had arched, such a delicious nightmare, inviting him to join her.

He usually came as a dream.

At least the first time.

A dream that lingered long past waking . . . like a deep, slow burning that could not be satisfied.

And when he'd finally left her, languid and sated with his memory, he'd waited in the woods behind the house.

He'd waited for the sun to come up and the house to be empty, and then he'd willed himself onto that balcony and let himself in through the sliding glass doors.

Her name was Lucy, he discovered.

*Lucy . . .*

He'd found it stamped on an airline ticket that she'd tossed on her dresser; he'd seen it written on a luggage tag still attached to a suitcase full of clothes.

*Lucy. Lucy Dennison.*

He hadn't expected an interruption. He'd paused and listened, mildly annoyed, as the back door unlocked, as the kitchen cupboards banged open and shut, as the cleaning lady made her slow, labored journey up the stairs and down the hall.

But still, he'd had time to walk around Lucy's room.

To touch Lucy's things.

And, in those last few seconds before taking his leave, to lie down . . . smiling . . . in Lucy's bed.

# 13

"Why don't *you* drive?" Angela insisted as she opened the garage door.

Lucy paused beside the little red Corvette, her eyes wide with feigned innocence. *Good one, Angela—now you can honestly say you didn't drive your car anywhere except back and forth to school.* "Me? Oh, no, I'd rather *you* did. I mean, if you've been having trouble with it—"

"The thing is," Angela said quickly, "is that I'm sort of getting a headache."

"Oh. Well then, maybe we'd better stay home."

"I can't. I mean, I shouldn't. I mean, I promised my friends—you know, I'm supposed to be working one of the booths tonight at the fair, so I have to at least show up and help."

Was she telling the truth? Lucy doubted it, but told herself it didn't matter anyway. What was more important right now was just getting out of the house and getting along with her cousin.

"So what exactly is this Fall Festival?" she asked, as Angela guided her through the neighborhood and toward the opposite end of town.

Angela slumped down in her seat and sounded bored. "It's the school's biggest fund-raiser, and they have it every year."

"That's it?"

"It's like a fair, okay?" The girl gave an exasperated sigh. "They do it every year. Anyone can participate, so the school rents space to set up booths and then we get to keep whatever money we make. Lots of people come in from other towns, and there's, like, this little carnival, and they have food and stupid crafts for sale, and dumb games and prizes and stuff."

Lucy was only half listening, driving with one hand, using the other to fiddle with the radio. "Sounds fascinating. So where do you work?"

"Hey, that's my favorite station!" Angela complained. "What do you think you're doing?"

"I just wanted to catch the news. Just for one second, okay?"

"*One.*"

"Thanks. Now . . . *where* do you work?"

"Pin the nose on the scarecrow."

"Really?" The announcer was highlighting the day's local headlines. Fall Festival . . . daycare facility closing . . . fender bender on the old highway. . . "You make scarecrows?" No mention of dead bodies, no girls in open graves, no murders in Pine Ridge. *I couldn't have imagined it all, could I? Did I imagine Byron, too? And the necklace in class . . . and the girl in the bathroom . . . and the scar on my hand—*

"Watch out!" Angela yelped. "What is *wrong* with you?"

Startled, Lucy swung the car back to her own side of the road. "Sorry."

"Well, it might help if you stopped looking at your hand and kept both of them on the steering wheel, for God's sake."

"Sorry." Lucy's brain struggled to reengage. "What were you saying about scarecrows?"

"I *said*, of course I don't make scarecrows. It's a *game*. You blindfold people and spin them

120

around, and then they have to stick this ridiculous nose on the scarecrow."

"Like pin the tail on the donkey?"

"Exactly. And if you get the nose in the right place, you win a prize. Except we use velcro, not pins."

"What kind of prize?"

Angela sighed. "A scarecrow doll, what do you think?"

"Well . . . it sounds kind of fun."

"Yeah, if you have no *life*. Turn here."

Lucy did as she was told. They followed a narrow strip of blacktop for about ten minutes, then turned off again onto an even narrower dirt road, this one winding off through thickly wooded countryside for several more miles.

"That's it up there," Angela finally announced.

To Lucy's relief she saw the fairgrounds up ahead, a noisy carnival bright with lights and busy with activity. Across the road and a good walk away stretched a large unlit field where kids with flashlights directed traffic and motioned them to their parking spot.

"Okay," Angela said, unstrapping her seat belt.

"Why don't we just meet back here about ten-thirty?"

Lucy looked doubtful. "You're sure that's enough time to . . . to not worry Irene?" she remembered to say. "I mean, how can you know for sure how long her meeting will be?"

"Trust me. It's a stupid disciplinary committee, and they never end before eleven. Night's the only time they can get everyone together without having *other* very important meetings to go to."

"What kind of discipline?" Lucy couldn't help asking.

"A bunch of stupid frat guys. They're always such jerks, and they're always in some kind of trouble. I mean, you'd think they'd learn by now that it's *not* cool to get drunk and act like total idiots in the cemetery."

Lucy's hand froze on the door handle. "What . . . about the cemetery?"

"Some guys went into the cemetery last night and got drunk and were messing around. And I guess somebody saw them and complained."

It was all Lucy could do to keep her voice casual. "What were they doing, do you know?"

"The usual stuff, probably. Breaking things . . . stealing things . . . spray-painting the headstones . . . just your usual damage to private property. Oh—and I always love this one—making out with their girlfriends on the graves."

"So . . ." Lucy could barely choke out the words, "it was just a . . . a joke?"

"Well, *they* thought it was. But they're gonna get suspended and their fraternity will get put on probation." Angela thought a minute, then gave a wry smile. "That's the part Irene really likes. The punishment part."

But Lucy wasn't listening anymore. As she got the door open and climbed out, her mind was spinning with rage and disbelief. *A joke! Kids drunk and playing pranks!* No wonder there hadn't been any news coverage . . . no murder investigations . . . no reports of missing girls . . . And all the agony she'd suffered . . . the terror . . . the guilt and regret and horror and—

"Are you coming?" Angela was waving at her from the other side of the car. "The Festival's *this* way. God, I can't believe they made us park way out here in all this mud!"

Yet that still didn't explain her encounter with Byron that morning, Lucy reminded herself, following Angela through the field. Still didn't explain the things he'd said . . . the things he'd known . . .

*Unless he was part of the joke, too. Unless he was there last night with those other guys, and he guessed I might come back this morning, and he wanted to scare me into not saying anything . . .*

"*If you tell anyone . . . you could die . . . they wouldn't believe you anyway . . .*"

"Did you hear me?" Angela snapped.

"What? Sorry—what?" *Still doesn't explain Byron . . . still doesn't explain a lot of things—*

"I *said*, let's just meet back here at the car. Are you *listening* to me?"

"Yes," Lucy murmured. "I'm listening. Ten-thirty. Here at the car."

She felt betrayed. Mortified and furious at being the butt of such a cruel, twisted joke. How those guys must be laughing at her right now—if, in fact, they even remembered the sick charade they'd carried out last night.

"Okay," Angela said. "See you later."

They parted at the main gate, but Lucy

stood on the sidelines for a moment, taking everything in. It was after six now, and the Fall Festival was in full swing. Angela was right about one thing, she noted—it seemed the whole town had turned out for the event—the whole town and a whole lot more. The place was packed with people in the mood for fun. Lines were already long at the concession stands, and the air throbbed with loud music and the wild rumble of rides, the carousel calliope, and barkers hawking games of various skills and staminas. Lucy could smell food from every direction—hot dogs, doughnuts, cotton candy, barbecue. For the first time in hours she actually realized how hungry she was; she'd barely eaten anything since yesterday.

She bought a greasy hamburger and a watered-down Coke and ate while she walked. It had been years since she'd been to anything like a carnival, and it brought back happy memories of her childhood, of her and Mom off together on their special adventures. Despite the tasteless food and poignant memories, she actually began to feel better. And despite the pain and embarrassment of her entire day, she felt herself almost smile.

She tossed her trash into a bin and kept walking, squeezing her way in and out through the crowds. The night was chilly, the breeze sharp but not unbearable in her flannel shirt and oversized parka. She was glad she'd opted to leave her purse at home tonight—with her money and ID tucked tightly into the pocket of her jeans, she felt a lot safer. *Safer . . . that's funny.* For some reason, the irony of that nearly brought another smile to her face.

She paused at a booth selling candy apples. She bought one and bit through the hard, sticky sweetness, and then she headed back into the crowd.

The slow, shivery prickle at the back of her neck had nothing to do with the cold.

Lucy stopped, and three people ran into her from behind. She felt a sharp burst of pain as her upper lip split between the candy apple and her two front teeth.

Mumbling apologies, she worked her way over to a booth and stood with her back to the wall. She could feel the blood swelling from the cut, and she wiped it carelessly with the back of her hand. Her eyes roamed anxiously over the teeming mobs of people.

*Someone's following me. I feel it.*

Just like last night . . . when she'd run from those footsteps . . . when she'd run from one nightmare, straight into another . . .

She didn't see anything suspicious, of course—in that solid mass of faces, how *would* she? And after all that had happened in the last two days, Lucy wasn't even sure how much she could trust her own instincts anymore.

She dabbed at the blood on her lip.

She took another survey of the crowd.

*You're imagining things. Enough's enough. Pull yourself together, for crying out loud.*

She was almost past the carousel when she saw him.

He was moving quickly, shoving his way toward her through the mob, and as she recognized his face, Lucy instantly turned and headed the opposite way.

"Lucy!" she heard him yell, but she didn't answer, didn't even acknowledge him, just kept walking.

"Lucy! Wait! We've got to talk!"

She thought she could outrun him, but Byron caught up with her easily, grabbing her arm and forcing her around. Dropping her apple, Lucy twisted furiously from his grasp.

"Haven't you done enough already?" she exploded.

The look he gave her was grim, his voice low and urgent. "Come on, we can't talk here—"

"You've had your fun, okay? Now leave me alone!"

"Fun? What *fun*? What is this—?"

"Those frat guys playing jokes at the cemetery—and you were there, too—that's how you knew I'd come back! Well, are you proud of yourself?"

"I don't have a clue what you're talking about, but please, just listen to me—"

"I've listened to you enough. Now I'm going."

With one smooth movement, Byron caught her shoulders and steered her over to a booth. Then, pinning her flat against the wall, he leaned down over her, his black eyes narrowed.

"There are things you need to understand."

"No, *you* need to understand!" Lucy tried to break free, but he only held her tighter. "If you don't leave me alone right now, I'm going to scream as loud as I can and have you arrested!"

"Look, I know you're scared—you have every right to be. What happened last night was horrible, and you have no reason in the world to trust me. But you *have* to. You *have* to meet me tomorrow—"

"I'm not meeting you anywhere—"

"—the old church—nine o'clock—"

She opened her mouth to scream. She felt his fingers dig into her shoulders as he gave her a firm, quick shake.

"You saw something today," he said. His lips moved soft against her ear; his voice dropped to a whisper. "When you touched the necklace, you saw something happen. *You* know it . . . and so do I."

This time when she struggled, he let her go. Lucy bolted into the crowd, frantically shoving her way through, not caring where she ran, only desperate to get away.

She looked back once and thought she saw him following.

Instinctively she veered from the midway, cut behind the Ferris wheel, and raced down a narrow path between two busy picnic shelters. It took her a minute to realize she'd lost him. Another minute to catch her breath and get her bearings. She bent over, hands on knees, and took deep gulps of air, waiting for her heartbeat to return to normal.

Then slowly she lifted her head.

*That smell . . .*

Frowning, Lucy glanced at her surroundings. It was darker back here, and though several groups of people had congregated nearby to socialize, the booths had thinned out, giving way to weeds and trash Dumpsters and a tall wire fence. *Great. I must be at the back of the fairgrounds.*

The night seemed colder. Without the insulation of the crowds, Lucy felt the sting of the wind and tugged her parka tight around her. Even the air felt different, she realized—softer and heavier and mysterious somehow, ripe with the scent of woods and fields and deep lake waters . . .

*And that other smell . . .*

She could feel her heart quickening again in her chest. Her throat constricting. The blood chilling in her veins . . .

*That other, familiar smell . . .*

That sweet, lingering smell that had filled her room and her bed.

# 14

She had to follow it.

Despite the sick fear coursing through her, Lucy knew she had no other choice.

She had to follow it, and she had to find it.

*But where?*

It didn't seem to be coming from one particular spot, or even from one specific direction, but rather permeated the air around her like a fine, invisible mist. Very deliberately this time, Lucy breathed it in . . . sweet like before . . . delicate like before . . . only this time stirring something deep within her, as though long-dulled senses were struggling to awake.

Several girls walked by and gave her strange looks. Didn't they smell it, Lucy wondered? *How can they not smell it?* Such an unusual fragrance . . . tantalizing . . . weaving its way through the festival, separate and distinct among the millions of other aromas hanging in the thick night air . . .

She didn't go back the way she'd come. Instead she passed bumper cars and a petting zoo, and then she began walking faster, making her way behind a barn where an auctioneer competed with enthusiastic bingo players. She could smell fried chicken and fried pies, popcorn and cotton candy, and still, *still*, that heavenly fragrance, wafting just out of reach . . .

She turned a corner and walked faster. Past country singers on makeshift stages. Games of darts. Tables of homemade pickles and jams. The smell was getting stronger now—she could feel that it was close. As she broke into a run, she suddenly spotted a big orange tent ahead of her, with a huge display of scarecrows around it.

*Scarecrows* . . .

She could see the whimsical sign over the entrance—PIN THE NOSE ON THE SCARECROW—and the boisterous line of kids waiting to take their turns. *Isn't this where Angela's supposed to be working?*

Mumbling apologies, Lucy pushed her way to the front. It didn't make sense, but the fragrance actually seemed *stronger* here, more tangible than any other place she'd been so far, almost as though she could reach out and touch it and hold it in her hand. If only she could find Angela, she was sure her cousin would confirm it—how could *anyone* forget that curious aroma once they'd breathed it in?

"Hey, get to the end of the line!" A solemn-faced girl stopped her at the door, holding up one hand while trying to blindfold two squirming kids with the other. "Aren't you a little old for this game?"

Lucy hurriedly identified herself. "Sorry, I'm Angela's cousin—Angela Foster? Do you know where she is?"

"I thought you looked familiar—you were in some of my classes today." The girl nodded, though her expression didn't change. "Angela's having a smoke."

"I really need to find her."

"Go around back. I just saw her talking to some guy out there a second ago."

*What a surprise.* "Thanks."

Lucy didn't waste any time. As she slipped around the side of the tent, she saw that it backed up to a fence, with just a narrow grassy space between. Thick woods pressed so closely from the other side that some of the trees hung over, their branches practically sweeping the ground. In spite of the festivities going on in front, it felt weirdly isolated here, shadowy and claustrophobic.

"Angela?"

Turning the corner, Lucy stopped. The light was dim at best . . . yet she thought she saw the glimmer of a cigarette at the opposite end of the tent.

"Angela? It's me . . . Lucy."

Without warning, something soft slid over her forehead . . . covered her eyes. With a startled cry, Lucy reached up and felt something like cloth—felt it being tied snugly at the back of her head—and realized it was a blindfold.

"Angela, cut it out! This isn't funny!"

"Did you come to play?" the voice whispered.

Lucy stiffened. She could *feel* someone now, a body standing close behind her, someone tall, someone strong, pressed lightly against her back.

Someone who *wasn't* Angela.

"This isn't funny," she managed to choke out. *Kids playing pranks! Friends of Angela maybe— or just a case of mistaken identity—that's it! They think I'm someone else—they must think I'm Angela—*

"I'm not Angela," she said, more forcefully this time. "You've got the wrong girl."

"On the contrary . . ." the voice murmured, "I've got *exactly* the girl I want."

Her body turned to ice. Her mind fought for calm. There were people only yards away, yet she was alone. She could scream, but she doubted anyone would hear her over the noise of the fair. Should she scream anyway? Try to run? She could feel his body, the lean, firm length of it, touching hers, yet not forcefully, *not threateningly*, she realized with slow surprise.

He wasn't even holding her.

He was only holding the blindfold at the back of her head, and as Lucy's heart hammered wildly in her chest, she tried to keep her voice even.

"I think you've made a mistake," she said. "I'm not from here, and I don't know anyone. I'm just trying to find my cousin."

"But you haven't. It seems you've found *me* instead."

Again her mind raced. Had she heard that voice before? Did she recognize it—*anything* about it? He was talking so softly, as though his lips barely moved . . . a low whisper from deep in his throat . . . warm and resonant . . . thick and smooth as . . . *what?*

Lucy's breath caught.

His hand slid leisurely down the back of her neck . . . lingered upon her left shoulder. Every instinct told her to break away—to tear off the blindfold and run—yet her body felt strangely paralyzed.

"Where's Angela?" she demanded. Her voice had begun to quiver, and she knew he could hear it, though she tried to disguise it with anger. "They said she was out here with someone—you must have seen her!"

Something brushed gently across her mouth.

"You're bleeding," he murmured.

She'd forgotten the cut on her upper lip, but

137

now she felt it swell . . . felt the tender skin split open. A warm drop of blood seeped out and began to trickle down.

Lips closed over hers.

A kiss so tender that time faded and stopped . . . so passionate, it sucked her breath away.

Lucy's senses reeled. Searing heat swept through her—pain and pleasure throbbing through her veins. With a helpless moan, she leaned into him and realized with a shock the kiss had ended.

At last she ripped the blindfold from her eyes.

The scent that had lured her here hung heavy in the night, though its fragile sweetness now held a trace of something more . . . something musky and faintly metallic . . .

Trembling violently, Lucy stared into the shadows.

But she was alone.

And she was cold.

# 15

*It can't be ten-thirty.*

As Lucy paused outside the scarecrow tent, she shook her wrist, tapped her watch, then held it to her ear and listened. Yes, it seemed to be working fine . . .

*But there's no way it can be ten-thirty already!*

"It's ten-thirty," the serious-faced girl said again. She was still trying to blindfold kids and maintain order at the same time, and as she frowned at Lucy, she added, "Did you have an accident or something?"

"Accident?" Lucy echoed. "No—what do you mean?"

"You're white as a sheet. And your lip's all swollen."

Lucy put a hand to her mouth and immediately winced. The skin on her lip felt pulpy and tender; she could feel a thin crust of dried blood.

"Are you sure Angela's not here?" she asked weakly.

"I told you, she left at ten-thirty. She said she had to meet her cousin—you—at the car."

"Right. Thanks anyway."

Her knees had turned to rubber. She wasn't sure she could walk three feet, much less the entire distance back to the parking lot. Her insides wouldn't stop shaking; she felt strangely disoriented. She'd stepped right into a dangerous situation with her eyes wide open, and she'd simply stayed in the middle of it, simply allowed the rest to happen. *What in God's name is wrong with me?*

She was probably lucky to be alive. The stranger—whoever he was—could have done a hundred horrible things to her—*and what did I do? I stood there and let him—I let him . . .*

Shame and confusion flushed through her. She could still feel his hand on her neck . . . on her shoulder . . . his body touching hers. And his kiss. That unexpected moment, senses reeling, his low whispery voice, intimate somehow, almost as though he knew her . . .

Her memory groped back—searching, searching. Trying to recall someone—*anyone*—he might have been. The guys from the cemetery last night? Had they followed her here, intent on more jokes? It seemed highly unlikely, given the disciplinary meeting tonight. Some guy at school she didn't know? *Byron?* Byron had a low, deep voice, but Byron had seemed agitated when she'd seen him earlier, he'd been tense and upset, and why follow her and frighten her when he'd already asked her to meet him secretly tomorrow?

*And what about the smell?*

Just thinking of that brought a fresh wave of panic. Because there *was* no explanation for it . . . none she could possibly think of . . . none that made any sort of sense. Before, she'd been almost willing to consider the air-freshener theory, but now . . .

As Lucy wandered out of the exit gates, she wished she had someone to leave with. The Festival was still in full swing, and only a handful of people were straggling toward the parking lot. Within minutes they'd located their cars, leaving her to walk the rest of the way alone.

The lights grew dim behind her. The noise began to fade. Out here in the field it was eerily quiet.

*Now where exactly did we park?*

Lucy stopped, cursing herself for her horrible sense of direction. It had gotten her in *major* trouble last night; she wasn't about to let it happen again. She glanced around, trying to find some sort of landmark, but all she could see was row after row of cars.

Why hadn't she thought of that earlier? Picked out a checkpoint to help her find her way back?

Frustrated, Lucy went on, trying to dodge puddles and sinkholes in the dark. Maybe Angela was in the car waiting for her—hadn't that girl at the tent said she'd already left?

"Angela!" Lucy called. "Angela! Are you out here?"

No answer. Just her own voice drifting back to her on the chilly breeze.

Lucy tried to walk faster. Why hadn't anyone thought to put temporary lighting out here? Why hadn't she thought to bring a flashlight?

Why hadn't she and Angela agreed to meet somewhere *inside* the Festival where it was bright and crowded and safe? *God, it's really, really spooky out here . . .*

She dug her hands in her pockets and felt the keyless entry to Angela's car. *Of course!*

Pulling it out, Lucy immediately hit a button. She could hear the blip of a horn in the distance, and she thought she saw the faraway flicker of headlights. *Well, at least I'm headed in the right direction.*

With the help of the mechanism, she finally spotted the Corvette, still about ten rows away, right on the end near the woods. The ground was even soggier out here, forcing her to walk close to the treeline. As she tramped her way through the weeds, she suddenly lifted her head to listen . . .

*What was that?*

She was sure she'd heard a sound just then . . . a faint scuffling off through those trees to her right. As though some animal were moving invisibly through the darkness . . .

*A deer. Just like last night when I thought I saw something, just a deer in the woods. That's all it is.*

Lucy stopped.

The noise stopped, too.

Very slowly she turned her head, eyes probing the bare, shifting branches of the trees . . . the deep, black underbelly of the forest . . .

*Or maybe it's a bear—bears live close to lakes, don't they? Or a wolf? Or—*

She broke into a run.

Because suddenly she didn't want to think what else it could be, this invisible presence keeping pace alongside her, skulking through the dark where she couldn't see.

It was last night's horror all over again.

With a burst of speed Lucy veered off between the cars, away from the woods, punching the entry over and over again, so the horn of the Corvette kept blasting and the headlights kept flashing on and off—on and off—

*God—oh God—help me—*

But it was *behind* her now—she could hear it thudding over the ground, *gaining* on her— coming closer—*closer*—

"Damnit, Lucy!" Angela yelled. "Wait up!"

With a cry, Lucy whirled around, just as her cousin closed the distance between them.

"Angela, you idiot! You scared the life out of me!"

"*I* did?" Braking to a stop, Angela tried to catch her breath. "*You're* the one running away— I thought something was *after* you!"

"Well, *I* thought something was, too!" Lucy exploded. "Were you in the woods just now?"

"What would I be doing in the woods?"

"I *heard* something in the woods."

"Oh, for God's sake—there's, like, about a *million* things you could've heard in the woods!" Angela gestured angrily toward the trees. "And where the hell have you been? I waited and waited by the car, but you never came. And *you* have the damn keys!"

Lucy thought quickly. There was no way she was going to mention what had happened back there at the tent. Not now . . . not ever.

"Sorry—I guess I lost track of time."

"I guess you did. Come on, let's get outta here."

Nodding, Lucy followed her to the car and got in, but not without a last anxious look at the woods. *Had* something really been there, following her? During the last few days, she'd lost so much faith in her instincts, she didn't know *what* to believe anymore.

She locked the doors and windows, but even after leaving the parking lot, Lucy still couldn't relax. The narrow, winding road was even harder to maneuver now that full night had fallen, and it took all her concentration to miss the endless potholes. Even Angela seemed edgier than usual, Lucy observed, watching the girl light up one cigarette after another, then mash them out half-smoked.

"Are you okay?" Lucy finally asked her.

Angela pointed to the clock on the dashboard. "I just want to get home before Irene does, that's all. Thank God she's going out of town tomorrow night, so I can have some peace. Lucy—hurry!"

"I'm hurrying."

"Well, hurry faster."

Glancing at her, Lucy sighed. "With all these stupid holes around here, if I hurry any faster, we're likely to bounce right off and—"

"*Look out!*"

As Lucy's eyes shot back to the road, she saw a quick streak of darkness in front of them. Jerking the wheel, she swerved the car sharply to the right, then slammed on the brakes as they slid dangerously along the shoulder. Angela gaped at her in alarm.

"Did you see that?"

"I saw *something*. But what was it?"

The Corvette had stopped now, and the two of them peered nervously out into the darkness. There was nothing on the road. Nothing moving in the beam of the headlights, nothing stirring at the sides of the car.

"We didn't hit anything, did we?" Angela finally asked.

"I don't think so. I didn't feel any sort of impact, did you?"

Angela shook her head. "It looked big. I mean, I only saw it for a second, but it was *big*."

"A deer, maybe?"

"No. It didn't seem like a deer. And it was so *fast*—just there and gone. I mean, what could move so fast that you can't even see it?"

"I don't know," Lucy answered uneasily. She

made a quick check in the rearview mirror. "Are you okay?"

"Yeah. I just hope my car is."

*For my sake, I hope so, too.* But the minute Lucy hit the accelerator, she heard the furious spinning of the tires. "Oh, great," she muttered.

"Oh, great, *what*?

"We're stuck."

"Stuck?" Angela seemed incredulous. "How can we be stuck?"

"Because there's about a foot of mud out there, and we drove right into it."

"No, *you* drove right into it." Shifting around, Angela unlocked her door. "If you've scratched anything out—"

"Stop," Lucy said. "Don't open it."

As Angela turned toward her in bewilderment, Lucy reached out slowly . . . put a hand on her arm.

"Lock your door," she whispered. "Now."

Even in the dim interior, she saw Angela go pale. She waited for the click of the lock, then leaned slowly toward the windshield.

"What is it?" Angela asked tightly.

"I saw something."

"Are you sure? Where?"

Lucy pointed. The car had skidded at a forty-five-degree angle, its headlights slicing off through the trees at the side of the road. As Lucy watched the illuminated pocket of woods, she felt a chill creep up her spine.

"Something's out there, Angela. It's watching us . . . don't you feel it?"

The girl's eyes widened slowly. Then she gave a forced laugh. "Come on, Lucy, you don't really expect me to fall for that, do you?"

But Lucy's tone was dead serious. "Do you have your phone with you?"

"Well, sure, but—"

"Call 911."

"Stop it. This isn't funny, and I don't believe you anyway."

"Well, you better believe me, because I'm telling you, there's something out there. And . . ."

As Lucy's sentence trailed off, Angela threw a quick, wary glance out her window. "Look. You're just shook up because of what happened. But I'm telling you, that thing was moving *fast*! Whatever it was, it's long gone by now—"

"Give me your phone," Lucy said tersely.

Before Angela could stop her, she grabbed the girl's purse and started rummaging through it, but Angela quickly snatched it back.

"What are you doing?" Angela snapped at her. "That's mine!"

"Your phone, Angela—your phone!" Lucy's voice was louder now, thin with rising panic. "Hurry up! Call 911! *Do* it, Angela, call for help!"

But she could see now that it was finally sinking in, Angela's eyes the size of saucers, her hands digging through her purse, tossing things out, searching for her cell phone. "This is sick, Lucy, do you hear me? This is *sick!*"

"It's coming closer! Make the call!"

Lucy's heart was racing. She could *feel* something out there—something furtive— something evil—a sense of danger so intense that every nerve vibrated with terror. It was standing just out of sight, standing just beyond the trees, one with the woods, one with the darkness, and it was waiting to strike . . . waiting to see what they would do . . .

"Oh, God," Lucy whispered, "Oh my God—"

"What is it!" Angela shouted, thoroughly frightened now. She dumped her purse upside down, the contents spilling everywhere, shaking it back and forth, helplessly close to tears. "I can't find it! I can't find my phone!"

"It's too late!" Lucy cried.

Something hit the side of the car. As both girls screamed, the Corvette rocked from the impact, and there was a frantic clawing at Angela's door.

"Get down!" Lucy yelled, even as she grabbed the girl and forced her to the floor.

"*What is it?*" Angela shrieked. "I can't see anything!"

Once more something lunged at the side. As the car swayed and slid, they heard a scratching at the door handle, as though something were trying to wrench it open. Terrified, Angela huddled beneath the dashboard, while Lucy whirled around just in time to see a dark shape dart behind the car. *Oh, God, it's coming to my side!* She leaned on the horn, the harsh sound splitting through the night, and then she gunned the motor.

The tires spun in the muck. Without even

thinking, Lucy shifted forward, then back, forward, then back—*tires whining, horn blasting, Angela screaming*—

The car lurched free.

Without warning, it popped from the mud and skidded sideways onto the road. Clutching the wheel for dear life, Lucy floored the accelerator, not stopping, not even slowing down till they'd reached the main highway once again.

"Stop it, Angela," she said then, quietly. "We're safe now."

"Safe?" The girl was practically hysterical. "*Safe?* How do you know we're safe? What *was* that thing?"

Lucy shook her head and said nothing.

"Then how do you know it didn't follow us? How do you know it's not sitting up there on the roof right now? Or—or—riding back there in the trunk?"

"Because it's not." Lucy's lips pressed into a tight line. "It's not. I just know."

As they paused at a stop sign, she shifted in her seat and took a long, deliberate look through every single window.

*How* do *I know?* she wondered. *How do I really know?*

There were houses around them now, and quiet, tree-lined streets.

And the peaceful silence of neighborhoods settled in for the night.

But Angela was crying.

And Lucy's heart was still beating wildly in her chest.

*How did I know that thing was out there to begin with?*

# 16

It was a miracle they got home before Irene.

The girls pulled into the garage with just minutes to spare, leaving no time to examine the car or discuss what had happened back there on that dark country road. Not that Angela would have wanted to anyway, Lucy figured—which was perfectly fine with her. Trying to rationalize it to herself was hard enough.

She stood in the shower, trembling beneath the hard spray of the water. Still badly shaken from the attack on the car . . . still badly frightened from her encounter with the stranger behind the tent. *Only frightened?* Again she berated herself for being so careless, for putting herself in such a dangerous situation . . . yet at the same time she could still hear that low, whispery voice . . . feel the gentle urgency of that kiss . . .

How could cold, stark fear be so alluring at the same time? She was furious with herself for even considering such a notion. *What's wrong with me?*

She turned the water as hot as she could stand it, washing her hair, her face, her lips, every inch of her body, as though she might be able to wash away every memory, every horror, every single event that had touched her in the last two days. All she wanted to do was crawl into bed and have a peaceful night of dreamless, uninterrupted sleep. So it surprised her when she heard a soft knock on her bedroom door about an hour later and saw Angela peek in.

"We need to talk," Angela said.

Lucy nodded and motioned her inside. She'd been sitting up, too, unable to relax; now she scooted over so Angela could plop down beside her. The girl's dark raccoon eyes had been wiped off for the night, her long hair braided down her back. She was wearing a polka-dot flannel nightshirt and looked almost normal.

"I can't stop thinking about what happened," Angela blurted out. Her expression seemed strained and almost embarrassed. Her hands twisted nervously in her lap. "What do you think that was? I mean . . . really?"

"I don't know. I've been thinking about it, too . . . and I honestly don't know."

"Well, it must have been a wolf," Angela announced flatly.

"Are there wolves around here?"

"Well . . . usually farther north, but sometimes they leave their territory, right? I mean, like if they're hungry, or certain areas get too populated, I've heard of animals doing that."

Lucy wanted to believe her. "It's possible, I guess."

"But . . . it could have been a bear, too, maybe," Angela mused. "I was thinking maybe it was wounded. When an animal's wounded, it makes them kind of crazy, and then they attack things they wouldn't normally attack, right? I mean, haven't you heard that?"

Lucy nodded. "It makes sense."

"So if something was hurt . . . and hungry . . . and smelled us in the car . . ."

Angela paused, her eyes almost pleading. "It *could've* happened that way. Right?"

"Sure. Sure it could."

"Great." Angela let out a huge sigh of relief. "And it's probably not a good idea to tell anyone else about it, do you think? Just so we don't cause a panic or something. And especially Irene. Because of her worrying, I mean."

"Absolutely. Our secret."

Another relieved sigh. Angela stretched her willowy limbs, then hopped off the bed.

"Great. Good night, then."

"Good night."

Mildly amazed, Lucy watched her go. How did Angela do it, she wondered? How could she make something go away so easily—or not even exist at all—just by refusing to accept it?

*But isn't that what you're doing?*

"No," Lucy mumbled to herself. "That's different."

*Is it?*

And in that very instant, razor-sharp images began strobing through her mind—images of Byron at the cemetery, Byron at the Festival, Byron trying to talk to her, to warn her about something: "I want to help you . . . some things take time to believe in . . . we don't have a lot of time . . . something happened . . . something important . . . touched you . . . was passed on to you . . . you need to understand . . ." As Lucy pressed her hands to her head, it was as if she could suddenly *feel* all those crazy puzzle pieces tumbling through her mind . . . falling into place . . . beginning to make a frightening kind of sense.

Could it possibly be true? Could there *honestly* be a connection between Byron's warnings and the bizarre events that had begun to darken her life?

"*. . . no reason in the world to trust me . . . have to meet me tomorrow . . .*"

"You're right," Lucy mumbled again. "I don't have the slightest reason to trust you."

"Did you say something?" Angela asked.

Lucy jumped and stared at the door. Angela was back again, propped in the threshold, smoking a cigarette and frowning at her.

"I didn't say anything," Lucy muttered.

Her cousin shrugged. "You'll need to get my car washed in the morning."

"*I* will?"

"Well . . . *yeah*. Irene didn't see it tonight 'cause someone picked her up and she didn't go in the garage. But tomorrow she'll probably be using her car—and if she sees the shape *my* car's in, she's bound to know we were out tonight."

"But what about the damage? How are you going to explain all those scratches?"

"Vandalism *happens* in the school parking lot, Lucy." Angela gazed down at the floor, her expression bland. "It happens all the time. So just take it to the car wash, okay?"

"And who was your servant this time last year?"

Angela rolled her eyes. "Very funny. Just do it?"

"No, I won't do it. If she sees your dirty car, too bad." Grumpily, Lucy stacked up her pillows and fell back on top of them. "And you can *stop* giving me all these excuses about Irene worrying—I heard you two this morning, and I know you're grounded."

Angela stared. A flush went over her face, though from anger or embarrassment, Lucy couldn't tell. She hesitated a moment, as if trying to decide what to do. Then with a sound of exasperation, she tossed her cigarette into the toilet, walked back to the bed, and flounced down on the edge.

"If you knew, then why'd you take me tonight?" she demanded.

"Because I thought it would help things between us. I wanted us to be friends."

"That's stupid. How could we ever be friends?"

"My point exactly. Which is why I'm not going to get your car washed tomorrow."

"If Irene finds out I left tonight, she'll cancel my credit cards!"

Lucy shrugged. She reached over and flipped off the lamp. Angela flipped it back on.

"Fine!" Angela pouted. "Look, if I tell you something *really* important and *really* secret about someone I met tonight, *then* will you wash my car?"

Lucy stared at her. Really *important*? Really *secret*? What could be more important than being stalked, than girls in graves, than hungry predators on lonely roads? What could be more secret than strangers with blindfolds, and painful visions, and disembodied voices in bathrooms?

She'd had enough. She switched off the light.

Angela switched it back on.

"Okay," Angela sighed. "I'll be your friend. Are you satisfied?"

"Angela, you don't know the meaning of the word."

The girl looked blank. "*Friend*? Or *satisfied*?"

"Neither one. Now get out of here and let me go to sleep."

This time when she reached for the lamp, Angela grabbed her arm. "I'll tell her *you* took my car. I'll tell her *you* stole my keys, and I didn't know anything about it. And if you deny it, I'll tell her you're lying . . . that you . . . that you . . . sneaked out to meet somebody!"

Lucy gave a humorless laugh. "Yeah, that's a good one, Angela, I'm sure she'll believe *that*. And while you're at it, be sure to tell her about the wild orgy I had out there behind the tents."

It slipped out before she even thought.

She saw Angela's eyes go wide, her face go red, saw her cheeks flinch as she drew in her breath.

"You bitch," she muttered. "You were *spying* on me!"

"What? Angela, no—I wasn't!"

Shocked at her cousin's reaction, Lucy tried to take her arm, but Angela was already halfway across the room.

"I was joking!" Lucy insisted. "I was joking about *myself*—I don't even know what you're talking about!"

"The hell you don't," Angela said furiously. "How long did you stand there watching, anyway? And it *wasn't* an orgy!"

"I wasn't watching anything! I was just making fun of myself!"

She saw Angela turn toward her then, a range of emotions flickering over the girl's face—indecision, guilt, embarrassment and the horrible realization that she'd just given herself away.

"Well . . . well . . . me, too!" she announced, with a forced little laugh. "*I* was just joking, too. I just wanted to see what you'd say."

Lucy stared at her as though she'd lost her mind. "Okay," she offered tentatively. "So we're even, right?"

"Right." The laugh again, almost brittle. "Okay, then. Great jokes. Good night."

"Good night." Lucy paused, then, "Angela?"

"What?"

"How late does Irene sleep on Saturdays?"

"Till around ten. Why?"

"I'll get your car washed. But I want to leave early, just in case she gets up."

"Like, how early?

"Like, before nine."

# 17

It was no problem slipping out of the house the next morning.

Everyone else was still asleep, and since Angela had already given her the keys and explicit directions to the car wash, Lucy was away in no time at all.

The car wash hadn't opened yet. Checking her watch, she saw that it was only eight-thirty, so she made a quick run through a fast-food drive-through, then sat in the parking lot, trying to digest both her food and her thoughts.

*This is really stupid. Byron probably won't even be there. And if I do go, and it really is another joke, I'll never be able to show my face anywhere in Pine Ridge again.*

But obviously he'd gotten there before her.

As Lucy drove slowly past the church, she noticed an old Jeep pulled alongside the curb in front, but not a soul to be seen. *Strange that Byron would park here in plain sight*, she found herself thinking. Especially since he'd made this meeting sound so secret and so mysterious . . .

Still, this *was* an abandoned church, and it *was* in an abandoned area—*not like there's going to be anyone around here watching us or wondering what we're up to*. Besides, seeing his Jeep out here in the open made her feel a whole lot safer.

Lucy parked, then made her way slowly up the crumbled walkway. The church had looked so spooky that night of the storm, and here in the daylight, it didn't look a whole lot better. Like the original section of the cemetery stretching off behind it, tall weeds had taken over, and shadows lurked beneath the gnarled branches of giant old trees. The steps to the door were rotted. The belltower didn't look at all sturdy. Several stained-glass windows were broken, and dead ivy crept over the walls.

It was very still. No breeze this morning, and frostily cold. Lucy's breath hung in the air as she glanced nervously back at her car. She'd parked close for a quick getaway. She told herself to go inside, then stopped with her hand on the door. *You're doing it again—walking right into an isolated, unknown place—have you completely lost your mind?*

When girls in *movies* did this, they always got killed, she reminded herself. But this wasn't a movie, this was real life—*my life!*—and she needed answers, and right now it seemed that Byron was her *only* chance at getting those answers.

She saw then that one of the large wooden doors was slightly open. That there were muddy footprints on the steps, leading inside.

Very slowly Lucy inched open the door. "Hello? Is anyone here?"

The silence was unnerving. Again she glanced back over her shoulder, but nothing moved within those calm, black shadows.

"Byron?" she called softly. "Hello?"

Lucy strained her ears through the quiet. Had the door creaked then, just ever so slightly? As though someone might be pushing it from the other side?

Instinctively she released it and stepped back. "Hello?"

Why wasn't he watching for her, why wasn't he out here waiting to see if she showed up? It had been *his* idea, after all—if he'd wanted her here so badly, why wasn't he coming out to meet her?

But it was very cold, she reasoned, and it made perfect sense that he'd probably go inside to wait. And these doors, made of such thick solid oak, surely muffled any sounds from outside. *Don't be so paranoid . . . Angela knows him . . . apparently all the girls at school are in love with him . . . it's not like he's some total creep that nobody's ever heard of . . .*

Still, Lucy suddenly wished she'd told somebody where she was headed this morning.

Just in case.

*Okay . . . here goes.*

She took a deep breath and yanked hard at the door. As it moved on rusty hinges, a low groan echoed back through the vast interior of the church.

She smelled dampness and old stone. Cold, stale air, long unbreathed, long undisturbed.

Shivering, Lucy stood there a moment, her eyes trying to adjust to the gloom. As the door swung shut with a dull thud, she moved farther into the vestibule.

"Byron?"

The church was still sadly, hauntingly beautiful. In the muted stained-glass light, Lucy could see saints gazing down at her from niches along the walls, their painted faces filled with loving concern. Wooden pews stood empty, sifted with dust, and high in the rafters of the arched ceiling, doves fluttered gently as she passed beneath them. Lucy walked slowly up the center aisle. She could see the main altar ahead of her, draped with a dingy white cloth, decorated with arrangements of long-dead flowers.

Despite the eeriness of the place, Lucy felt strangely fascinated. She stopped before the altar, trailing her fingers over the musty cloth, over faded droplets of candle wax, over brittle chrysanthemum petals. Even her heart seemed to echo in here; she could hear the faint beat of her pulse.

*God, it's so cold . . .*

Blowing on her hands, Lucy turned in a slow circle and glanced uneasily at her surroundings. Was it her imagination, or had the temperature dropped about ten degrees just since she'd walked through the door? *You* are *imagining things.* Yet as she blew once more on her hands, she could see her breath forming, a soft vapory cloud right in front of her face.

"Byron?"

Her own voice whispered back to her from the shadows.

The doves stirred restlessly with a muffled beating of wings.

"Come on, Byron, if you have something to say, you'd better say it—*now!*"

*This is stupid. He's not here, and he's obviously not going to show up, and all you're doing is creeping yourself out.*

With growing anxiety, Lucy gnawed on a fingernail. *Not again . . . not again! What did you expect, anyway? Haven't you learned your lesson by now?*

But she'd wanted this time to be different— she'd wanted so *much* to believe that Byron could help her. She'd wanted to *prove* to herself once and for all that it wasn't just her, that there were reasons and answers and explanations for the things that were happening, that she *wasn't* just making up dreams in her mind—

*Something's here.*

Lucy gasped as a sliver of dread snaked its way up her back and lodged at the base of her neck.

*Something's here!*

Instantly her eyes swept over the walls and ceiling, the massive wooden cross above the altar, the partially shattered glass of the crucifixion behind it, the confessionals in the darkened aisles along the side . . .

*The confessionals . . .*

A soft sound slithered through the church. A sound like . . . *what*? A sigh of wind? A flurry of feathers? Or . . .

*Breathing.*

Lucy's body stiffened, every nerve electrified. *No, it can't be . . . there's no one here . . . no one . . . no one . . .*

Yet she could feel herself moving across the cold stone floor, moving steadily toward the confessionals, almost as though something were *drawing* her forward, some force against her will.

She tried to stop, but she couldn't. Tried to resist, but the pull seemed only to grow stronger.

She stopped outside one of the doors.

*Byron?*

She tried to whisper, but the words stuck soundlessly in her throat. She could see the door cracked open, barely an inch, but she couldn't see what was inside. And yes—*yes!*—there was the sound again . . . like the faintest breath, the most feeble attempt at a sigh.

Steeling herself, Lucy jerked open the door.

The space was cramped and narrow, murky with shadows, and as she stepped tentatively across the threshold, she could see the small priest's window to the left, the bit of screen and gauzy curtain concealing it from the other side, the kneeler beneath it on the floor.

The compartment stank of mildew; it was covered thickly in dust.

No sins had been confessed here for a long, long time.

*See? Nothing. Just your imagination.*

Almost weak with relief, Lucy turned to walk out.

And saw the door slowly creak shut.

Startled, she stared at it a moment, then gave it a push. The door didn't move. She pushed harder, then leaned into it with her shoulder. It wouldn't so much as budge.

*That's strange . . .* She couldn't remember seeing a latch on the outside of the door, and it hadn't stuck when she'd yanked it open. Trying not to panic, Lucy tried it again, harder this time, then harder still, but the door refused to give. Dust swirled into the air, choking her, irritating her eyes. She yelled and pounded on the walls. The space seemed to be growing smaller, the dust thicker, the high walls closing in—*Oh God—let me out of here!*

The thought briefly shot through her mind that no one would find her, maybe not for days and days, maybe not ever—she'd simply die here in the dark, in this tiny dark space, trapped in an upright coffin.

"Byron!" Lucy screamed. There was a *car* parked outside, for God's sake, *somebody* must be around! "Please! Please, somebody, I'm stuck in here—*let me out!*"

"Have you come to seek God's forgiveness, my child?" the voice murmured.

Lucy went cold. Her fists froze upon the door, her mouth gaped in a silent scream.

Her eyes turned fearfully to the wall . . .

She could see the priest's window, only now it was open. The curtain had been pulled back, and beyond the small screen was the dim outline of a face.

A face . . . yet somehow . . . and even more terrifyingly . . . *not* a face.

"Who are you?" Lucy choked out. Her back was against the door now, her knees so shaky she could hardly stand. It took every ounce of willpower to focus on that window and the featureless profile beyond. "*Who are you?*"

"Your salvation."

And she *knew* the voice, and he seemed to be all around her now, in the air, in the dust, in the echo of her heartbeat, in the thoughts inside her head, in the ice flowing through her veins . . .

"You were at the Festival," she realized. "Behind the tent, you were the one—"

"Meant to save you," he whispered. "No more sorrow . . . no more pain. Reprieve from the lifetime of loneliness that awaits you. Redemption from yourself."

"Please—"

"I know how lost you've been without your mother."

Tears filled Lucy's eyes . . . trickled slowly down her cheeks. "Why? Why are you doing this?"

"It's no longer a matter of why. It's a matter of when. Of how."

"I don't understand. I don't know you . . . I haven't done anything to you. Why won't you just leave me alone?"

"But you *have* done something to me. We have a connection, you and I." The voice sounded mildly amused. "So let me ask you again . . . have you come to seek God's forgiveness?"

"Forgiveness for what?" she cried desperately.

"For the places your heart will take you . . . where your soul cannot go."

Without warning the door came open.

As Lucy stumbled out into the aisle, she grabbed the door of the priest's compartment and flung it open.

But the darkness inside was empty.

And the dust not even disturbed.

# 18

Lucy stood there, unable to move.

Like a distant observer, she watched herself staring into the confessional, felt her slow-motion shock and disbelief—yet at the same time, felt oddly detached from reality. As she wheeled around to run, a tall figure suddenly materialized from the shadows behind her, sending her back with a scream.

"Hey, sorry!" he laughed. "Didn't mean to scare you! Guess I should've yelled or something, right?"

Before she could even react, the young man stepped closer, right into a narrow beam of light angling down from an overhead window. He had a friendly, boyish, dirt-streaked face and an equally friendly smile. Mid-twenties, probably—broad, solid shoulders . . . slender build . . . thighs and arms leanly muscled beneath skintight jeans and the pushed-up sleeves of a grimy sweatshirt. His eyes were deep blue, fringed with long dark lashes. His thick brown hair, though dusted with cobwebs, still showed a few golden streaks of fading summer sun. He was slightly out of breath and carrying a large cardboard box, which he immediately wrestled down to the floor.

Lucy gazed at him with open—and hostile—suspicion.

The young man merely grinned. "Is there something I can help you with?"

Lucy's gaze hardened. The stranger seemed oblivious.

"Matt," he said, reaching toward her. "Oh, wait. Sorry." He swiped his hand across the back of his jeans, then offered it again. "Matt. Well . . . *Father* Matt, actually. Well . . . Father *Matthew*, really. But you can call me Matt."

Lucy was dumbfounded. "You're . . . a *priest?*"

"Hmmm . . ." He glanced around in mock concern. "Should I apologize?" And then, as she continued to stare at him, he added, "Hey, it's okay. I'm out of uniform. And you are—?"

Lucy said nothing. Matt gave a solemn nod.

"Speechless," he said.

"Lucy," she finally whispered.

"Nice to meet you, Lucy. But I hope you weren't planning on confessing anything today, because as you can see, we're slightly out of service at the moment. Have been, actually, for years."

Lucy's eyes narrowed. Was this guy for real? Was he telling the truth? She tried to concentrate on his voice . . . what would that voice sound like, low and deep and whispering?

"Listen, are you okay?" Matt's smile seemed genuinely concerned. "Would you like to sit down?"

"Where were you just now?" Lucy murmured.

She saw his smile falter, but only for a second. "Sorry?"

"Just now. Where were you?" Her voice was trembling from aftershock; she fought to keep it steady. She watched his glance flicker toward the confessionals . . . the altar . . . the empty pews behind him.

"Just now?" This time he gestured vaguely with one arm. "Going through some closets in back. Sorry, I didn't know you were here— otherwise I'd have been a lot more hospitable."

"You didn't hear me yelling?"

"Yelling?" Matt frowned. Then, as though a thought had just occurred to him, he pulled some headphones from the box and dangled them in front of her. "I've been lost in Mozart. Just pulled these off when I saw you standing here. What were you yelling about?"

"I was . . ." Lucy's mind raced. "I was yelling . . . to see . . . if anyone was here."

Matt's smile widened. "Well, now you know."

*He must be telling the truth . . . he wouldn't have had time to run from the confessional and grab that big box from somewhere and come back without me seeing him or hearing him or—*

"Is it my face?" Matt asked, deadpan. "Or are you having a religious experience?"

Lucy snapped back to attention. "What?"

"You're staring at me like I have horns growing out of my head or something."

Flustered, Lucy looked away. "Are you alone here?"

"Alone?"

"Is there someone else here with you?"

Matt's eyes made a quick survey of the church. "Not that I know of. Why?"

"Nothing . . . I . . . I just thought I heard something, that's all."

"Now you're making *me* nervous," he teased, though once more his eyes swept the room. "It was probably just me rummaging around back there. There's a major echo in this old place, and—"

"No. No, it . . . it wasn't like that. It was a voice."

"A voice? Well, what did it sound like?"

Lucy shook her head. He *seemed* sincere, but how could she know for sure? And if he really *was* who he said he was, then how could she explain something so totally unbelievable? For an instant she dug deep into her memory, trying to recall the exact sound, the exact tone of that voice in the confessional . . . that voice at the fair. It *could* be Matt's voice disguised . . . just like it could be *anybody's* voice disguised.

*Or maybe it wasn't disguised at all . . .*

Lucy wrapped her arms about herself, suppressing a shudder. "I must have imagined it. I thought I heard someone."

This time Matt turned and took a good hard look toward the entrance. "Well, I didn't lock the door behind me this morning. So I guess it's possible someone could've sneaked in. Kind of like you did."

This seemed to amuse him, especially when a slow flush crept over Lucy's cheeks. Quickly she stammered out an explanation.

"I was . . . *supposed* to be meeting someone."

"Ah. A clandestine rendezvous. How intriguing."

Flushing hotter, she mumbled, "It's not what you think."

"No? And how do you know what I think?" Matt's eyes sparkled with humor, and he ran one hand back through his hair. "Maybe it was this friend of yours you heard. Maybe he really did show up, but he thought you weren't here."

*And maybe I was a total fool for believing what Byron said and for coming here to meet him.* "I don't think so."

"Well, maybe it was burglars," Matt said practically. "And when they realized there wasn't anything to steal, they got disappointed and left."

Lucy was ready to change the subject. "What happened to this place, anyway?"

"Don't you know?"

"I'm not from here. I just came a few weeks ago, to live with my aunt."

"I see." Matt leaned back against the wall, crossing his long legs, folding his arms casually across his chest. For a second Lucy thought he was going to ask her some personal questions, but instead he said, "All I know is that a bigger, fancier church was built in the center of town, and that's when this place became . . . shall we say . . . a sort of ecclesiastical warehouse."

"So you must remember when this place was really beautiful."

Matt shook his head. "Actually, no—I'm not from Pine Ridge either. And in *theory*, I'm only supposed to be here temporarily."

"In theory?"

"Well, that's what Monsignor's telling Father

Paul at the moment. That I'm only here till he gets back on his feet."

"Who's Father Paul?"

"The priest at the *real* church," Matt explained. "He's *old*—no, let me rephrase that—he's *ancient*. And very set in his ways. He's been refusing to take on an assistant for years, but I guess you could say he finally got a dose of Divine Intervention."

"How's that?"

Matt chuckled. "He fell down a flight of stairs." Then, at Lucy's look of alarm, "No, no, he's *fine*—but now that he's got a broken leg, it's forced him to slow down and listen to reason."

"And how does he feel about *you* being here?"

Again Matt laughed. "Let's put it this way. Since he's been here for about a hundred years and has a very particular way of doing things, I *obviously* am a complete and total moron. And just trying to wade through his particular way of doing things is probably going to take me the rest of my natural life."

Pausing, he gave Lucy a helpless look

"*If* he doesn't kill me before then. Like right now, I'm supposed to be looking for some statues he *swears* are stored down here in one of the cellars. But I can't seem to find the right doors—*or* the right keys."

He looked so distressed that Lucy couldn't help smiling. But as she caught a sudden movement from the corner of her eye, she gasped and spun toward it.

"Hey, easy," Matt soothed her, "it's just one of the cats."

"Cats?"

"Yeah, there're a bunch of them in here—the cleaning lady's always bringing them in. Just call it environment-friendly rodent control."

As Lucy nodded uncertainly, he frowned and lifted a hand to her forehead.

"You know, Lucy, maybe it's just this bad light, but you sure don't look like you feel very well. Why don't you sit down, and I'll get you some water."

His touch was firm, but gentle. His fingertips skimmed lightly over her skin and carefully brushed a strand of hair from her eyes. With no warning, Lucy felt a strange, slow warmth pulse softly at her temples . . . flow like liquid to the back of her brain . . .

*Flowing . . . flowing . . . blood flowing . . . a dark red pool of blood on . . . on . . . a floor and something—something—*sharp!*—*cutting!*—pain and blood and anger—*

"You hurt yourself," Lucy said. She stepped back and saw a look of dismay on Matt's face. "You hurt yourself, and it was very painful, and you bled for a long time."

The throbbing in her head was gone now, but her body felt shaky and drained. She watched as Matt frowned at her, as he lowered his hand. As he stared at the long, narrow cut on his palm and cautiously flexed his fingers.

"Well, yeah, but it's okay now," he assured her. "I mean, it happened a few days ago . . . it's not infected or anything, if that's what you're worried about."

Lucy took another step back, her emotions whirling. *He thinks I saw it*, she realized, *only I didn't see it, not the way he thinks—not with my eyes, but somewhere inside my head—and not* exactly *what happened—just those flashes again—flashes and feelings and colors and—*

"—broken glass," Matt was saying, as she tried to quiet her mind, focus in, act normally. "From one of those windows . . . it sliced right through me. It hurt like hell."

"I'm . . . I'm sorry." Flustered, Lucy pointed to the front of the church. "I'm feeling better now. I need to go."

But she could tell Matt wasn't convinced, even as she began walking away from him.

"What about your friend?" he asked her. "Is he supposed to pick you up?"

Lucy shook her head.

"Well, how are you getting home?"

"I have a car."

Look," Matt said kindly, "I'd be more than happy to drive you. Someone can come back later for your car."

"No. I'm fine, really. But thanks."

She was almost outside when he stopped her. She heard him call her name, and she turned to see him running after her, waving something in his hand.

"Lucy," he said again, catching up with her at the door. "I think you must've dropped this."

Lucy stared down at the thing he was holding. And felt her eyes widen in alarm.

"I don't know anything about it," she said quickly. *Too quickly?* Because she could see the way he was looking at her now, that quizzical expression on his face, as though he *knew* she was lying, as though he *knew* and was waiting for her to confess . . .

She backed away, trying to put distance between them. "Sorry. It's not mine."

"Oh, that's too bad." Matt shrugged. "I found it on the floor near the altar. I just assumed it must be yours."

He gazed down at the necklace he was holding.

A single strand of tiny green beads.

"No," Lucy said again breathlessly, "no, it's not mine."

"Well, I guess I'll just leave it, then. Just in case whoever lost it comes back."

"Yeah. Maybe."

She hurried down the walkway, and she didn't once look back.

But if she had, she would have seen him still standing there . . . watching . . .

Watching her . . . even as he slipped the necklace casually into his pocket.

# 19

Lucy couldn't get into the car fast enough.

She locked the doors and fumbled the key into the ignition, turning it, pumping the accelerator, but the engine only coughed uselessly.

"Damn!"

Leaning forward, she rested her head on the steering wheel and alternately struggled to catch her breath and not give in to tears.

So Byron *had* been at the church. He *must* have been; otherwise, how would the necklace have ended up there? Yet she couldn't imagine him leaving it behind. Even from her brief encounters with Byron, it was obvious the necklace was important to him, that it tied in somehow to that girl in the cemetery. And Lucy had definitely experienced something when she'd handled it yesterday—and Byron had definitely known.

*What if something's happened to him?*

A million thoughts ran through her mind. Could he have left it as a message to her? A warning? Or could it even have been some sort of trap? But a trap for what?

Like so many other things these last few days, it didn't make any sense to her, didn't fit into any concept of logic or reality.

Lucy groaned and lifted her head. As she reached out again for the key, she suddenly saw a movement in the rearview mirror. With a shocked cry, she spun around just as Byron clamped a hand down on her shoulder.

"Ssh . . . it's just me," he said tightly. "Look, I really need your help."

Furiously, Lucy flung his hand away, then fixed him with a glare.

"What the *hell* do you think you're doing!" she shouted. "You nearly gave me a heart attack!"

"Then lock your doors next time." He frowned back at her. "Are you listening to me? The necklace is gone."

"*What?*"

Byron's jaw stiffened. "It was gone when I got home last night."

"After the Festival?"

At Byron's nod, Lucy gave him a puzzled look. "But I just saw it."

"What do you mean you just saw it?"

"In there. Matt has it."

"Who?"

"Matt . . . uh . . . Father Matt," Lucy stammered.

"Who's that?"

"The priest. The new priest at the church."

"*What* new priest?"

Lucy bristled. "How should I know? Father Paul's new assistant—he's here helping out because Father Paul broke his leg."

"So that's who was in there," Byron muttered. "Well, did you get it from him?"

"No, I didn't get it from him. It's not my necklace. Why would I get it from him?"

Facing forward again, she redirected her glare to his reflection. She saw him rub a hand across his forehead; she saw the visible strain upon his face.

"Are you sure it was the same necklace?" He sounded almost accusing. "That just doesn't make sense."

"He said he found it on the floor."

"But that's impossible, I didn't even *have* it when I was in the church."

Lucy couldn't keep the sarcasm from her voice. "And speaking of that—why exactly *weren't* you in there? If you were supposed to be *meeting* me?"

"Because I heard someone come in. Because I didn't know who it was, and I wasn't sure it was safe."

"Well, you were right. It *wasn't* safe. But, hey, it wasn't *you* being scared to death, so why were you even worried about it?"

"What do you mean?" His glance was sharp. "What happened?"

"I don't *know* what happened!" Lucy could hear herself getting louder, could hear the edge of hysteria in her voice, but couldn't seem to stop herself. "I don't know why I even *came* here today! I don't know why I'm even *speaking* to you! Get out of my car!"

"Drive," he said.

"*What?*"

"Just drive. I'll tell you where."

"No, I'll tell *you* where! *No*where! I'm not moving one inch till you get out of this car."

"I'm not getting out until we talk." She felt his hand on her shoulder again. His voice softened, tired. "Please. You have to listen to me. You're the only one I can talk to."

Lucy lowered her head. She chewed anxiously on her thumbnail, then shot him another look in the mirror.

"I can't go. The car won't start."

Byron stared at her a long moment. Then a faint smile played at the corners of his mouth.

"You flooded the engine, that's all. Try it again."

This time when she tried to start it, the car sprang to life. Grumbling under her breath, Lucy headed off down the street.

"So what happened in the church?" Byron asked again. He'd scooted closer to her now, leaning in between the bucket seats, and Lucy could feel the faint pressure of his arm against hers.

"If I tell you," she answered wryly, "you won't believe me."

"I doubt that. Turn here."

"Where are we going?"

"Someplace private."

Lucy cast him a sidelong glance. "I can't believe I'm doing this. Why should I even trust you?"

"Because you have to trust somebody. Because I'm guessing your life's suddenly been turned upside down."

Lucy tried to keep her expression blank, tried to ignore her shiver of apprehension. "I'm not sure that's an answer."

"Okay. Then for the same reason I have to trust you," Byron replied flatly. "We're the only ones who know about the cemetery. The only ones who know that something happened."

Lucy gave a terse nod. "So you're telling me that what I saw *wasn't* the fraternity prank I heard about. That what I saw was—"

"Real. Yes."

"So that girl . . ."

"Was murdered."

"But . . . by *who*?"

"That's why we have to get the necklace back. So you can tell us."

"So *I* can tell us? Tell us *what?*"

"Who killed her."

"Oh, now, wait a minute—"

"Hey, watch the road," Byron warned, as the car veered sharply into the wrong lane. "I'll tell you everything when we get to where we're going. Even the stuff you won't want to hear."

Lucy gripped harder on the steering wheel. "And how do I know *you* didn't kill her?"

She hadn't known she was going to say it; the words burst out before she could stop them. She felt his steady gaze upon her, and her heartbeat quickened in her chest.

"Just drive," he said tersely.

Yet with a start, Lucy realized how very sad he sounded.

Following his directions, she drove several miles outside of town, then turned off onto an isolated road that followed the curve of the lake. After another half hour, they finally pulled up to a cabin nestled among tall green pines, with a breathtaking view of the water.

"This is so beautiful," Lucy murmured. "Is it yours?"

"No. Somebody's summer home."

"Somebody's?"

"It's locked up now for the winter, but I have the key."

"And how did you manage that?"

Byron turned and glanced out the back windshield. With a twinge of uneasiness, Lucy wondered if he was afraid they'd been followed.

"Just park the car," he told her. "Over there behind those trees."

It wasn't until they were inside—door securely locked and bolted—that Byron seemed to relax a little. The cabin was very cold, and as Lucy stood rubbing her hands together, Byron went into the adjoining room, returned with a quilt, then motioned her into a rocking chair beside the fireplace.

Lucy sat. "Will you please just tell me what's going on?"

"Do you promise to believe me?"

"Probably not."

She thought a reluctant smile might have tugged at his mouth. He tossed her the quilt, then waited while she snuggled beneath it.

*This is insane*, Lucy thought. *This is completely insane. With everything else that's happened to me, I can't believe I'm sitting here in a cabin in the woods with some stranger who's asking me to trust him. If he murders me right now in this rocking chair, then I guess I deserve it.*

As Byron leaned down over her, her breath caught in her throat. His stare held her for an endless moment and then he slowly straightened.

"You still don't trust me. I see it in your eyes."

Lucy didn't miss a beat. "I don't believe you can see anything in my eyes. When I first saw you in the cemetery, you knew my mother had died, that I was alone. But you go to school with Angela—anyone could have known that."

"You're right. Anyone could've known, because Angela told everyone you were coming. Except . . ."

"Except what?"

Byron stepped closer. "Except I didn't know what you looked like. I'd never seen any pictures of you . . . never heard any descriptions. And I didn't know when you came to the cemetery that morning, that you were Angela's cousin."

Again that tiny shiver of apprehension; again Lucy tried to ignore it. "So . . . what are you trying to prove? That you have some sort of supernatural power? That you can know things about people just by staring at them?"

She wanted to laugh, to make light of it, but she suddenly realized that Byron had taken her hand, her right hand, that he was lifting it toward him and placing it over his heart.

"What do you feel?" he murmured.

And without warning, a whole range of emotions surged through her—*warmth . . . gentleness . . . fear . . . pain . . . sorrow*—all in a split-second rush that made her numb, that made her dizzy—*anger . . . loss . . . love*—

With a cry, Lucy jerked her hand from his grasp and cradled it against her chest, staring at him with wide, shocked eyes.

"You've been given a gift," Byron said solemnly. "And your life will never be the same."

# 20

"Do you think this is easy for me either? Having to say all these things to you—somebody I just met? And knowing how crazy it all sounds? And knowing—*understanding*, even—that the last thing in the world *you* want to do is *believe* me?"

Byron stopped . . . shook his head. There was bitterness in his tone.

"And why *would* you believe me? I mean, why would anyone believe *any* of this?"

Lucy couldn't do anything but stare. She watched as he crossed to the other side of the room, as he began pacing, slowly, back and forth between the fireplace and the door.

"That night at the cemetery," Byron's voice was low. "Try to think, Lucy. Try to remember."

But still Lucy sat there, paralyzed.

"Remember when I told you that something had been *passed on*?" Byron asked her.

At last she managed a nod.

"This gift you have . . . I think it was passed on to you from the girl who died. I suspected it . . . but I wasn't really positive till you picked up the necklace in class yesterday."

As if from a distance, Lucy heard herself ask, "I don't understand. Not about any gift . . . not about the necklace—"

"It was *her* necklace. She never took it off. So I know the only possible reason she did was to leave a clue behind. To try and tell me who killed her. To tell *you* who killed her."

"No. No . . . wait a minute. This is too much, this is—"

"True." Byron paused and shot her a level glance. "It's *true*, and no matter how much you want to forget about it, you *can't*. You have a responsibility now. You have—"

"A responsibility to who?" Lucy's voice went shrill with anger. "I don't have any responsibility to *anybody*—not to *you*—not to—"

"She had powers," Byron insisted. "She had powers nobody understood—and most people didn't believe in. And she used them for good, and she used them to help others when she could. But at the same time, she suffered for them her whole life. And now—now she's given them to you."

Lucy's lips parted soundlessly. For a second, Byron seemed to recede into some black void, then reappear again at the side of her chair.

"She could sense things," he said urgently. "See things that had already happened— sometimes even things that *hadn't* happened yet. By touching. Do you understand?"

Lucy shook her head. She wished he would stop talking, would leave, would just go away, but he knelt on the floor in front of her, where she couldn't ignore him.

"It didn't happen every single time—that's not the way it worked. But when it *did* happen, it was very powerful. She could never anticipate when the visions might come—sometimes they came from a person, sometimes from an object, just some little thing you'd never even think about."

Again Lucy shook her head. "So these visions she'd have . . . what were they, exactly?"

He stared at a spot beyond her, deep in thought, choosing his words carefully. "When she tried to describe it to me, she always said there weren't complete pictures. More like . . . like quick images or feelings. Sometimes colors or smells or sounds. She said it was like all her five senses had been peeled open, and raw, and they just kept absorbing all these impulses, with nothing to protect them."

His focus shifted back to her. Lucy saw his face through a fine mist and realized that tears had filled her eyes.

"Oh my God," she whispered. "Yes . . . it *is* like that . . ."

"You mean . . . like when you held the necklace?"

Without answering, she began to rock . . . a slow, gentle rhythm of self-comfort.

"Why'd you go there that night?" Byron asked quietly.

Lucy shut her eyes . . . tried to will the pain away.

"Please tell me, Lucy."

And so she did . . . recounting every moment from the time she'd left the house till Angela picked her up and took her back to Irene's. She told him everything, still feeling as though this were all some strange, distorted nightmare . . . still wishing she'd wake up, safe and warm in her mother's home. Still wondering why she was taking a chance with this mysterious young man she didn't know . . . why she was here trusting him and believing him, and in some painful way, feeling so grateful for his company . . .

And when she'd finally told her story, she realized that he'd taken her hand . . . spread her fingers wide apart . . . was gazing down at the tiny crescent scar upon her palm.

"She had a scar just like this," he said, not meeting Lucy's eyes. "In the same spot . . . on the same hand."

"It hurt," Lucy acknowledged numbly. "When she grabbed me . . . the pain I felt was unbearable—not like anything I'd ever felt before."

Nodding slightly, Byron placed her hand on the arm of the rocking chair. "I was supposed to meet her that night. She'd been away, and I hadn't seen her in nearly a year. Then I got this message from her—just out of the blue. Something important, she said. She told me to come alone, she'd be waiting at the old church. I could tell from her note that she was really scared. Only . . . she never showed up."

"So . . . I just happened to be walking past there at the same time?"

"I think the person following you that night was me."

Byron rocked back on his heels, his expression thoughtful. "I'd just gotten to the church when I saw you running away. And it was storming so bad, I couldn't really see anything. For a minute I thought it might be her, so I went after you—but then you turned under the streetlight. And when I realized it wasn't her, I went back."

"And that's when I ran into the cemetery. Because I thought you were stalking me."

"I should have known it was something bad." Byron's eyes were as hard as his voice. "When she didn't show up on time, I should have left right away—I should have looked for her then. But I just kept thinking maybe it was the storm, she was having trouble getting there, but that she'd *be* there, just five more minutes, she'd *be* there . . ."

He paused. Drew a sharp breath.

"I don't think I wanted to believe it. Even when I got in my van and started driving around, looking for her. I didn't want to believe something had happened to her. And that's when I saw you again."

"Me?"

"You were coming out of the cemetery, and you ran across the street to use the phone. And you looked terrified."

Lucy's heart gave a sickening lurch. How easily those feelings of terror returned, just from talking, just from remembering. She watched as Byron stood up and walked to the window. He propped his hands upon the sill and leaned forward, his shoulders stiff with tension.

"I knew," he mumbled. "I mean, there you were, scared and muddy and soaking wet—and suddenly I just *knew*. I knew it had something to do with her."

For several long moments there was quiet between them. Only the patient creak of the rocking chair upon the wooden floor. The muted songs of birds outside the windows. Until at last Byron spoke again.

"I tried to get over to you . . . to see if you needed help. But by the time I got the van turned around, you were gone. So I went back to the cemetery. And I looked for her." Byron's head lowered. "I never found her."

Lucy stopped rocking. She stared at his back with a puzzled frown. "But when I saw you the next morning—the things you said—how could you have known those things if you never found her? If you weren't actually there?"

"Because she told me."

"She . . ." Lucy sat straight in her chair. The quilt slid down to her waist, and she impatiently pushed it aside. "What do you mean, she told you—what are you saying?"

"In a dream that night. She told me in a dream."

He turned around to face her. As Lucy held his steady gaze, she slowly shook her head.

"You know something, Byron . . . you're asking me to believe a *lot*."

"Haven't you ever had a dream so real, you knew it was *more* than a dream?"

"Yes, but . . ." Lucy's voice trailed off. Until that moment she'd almost forgotten her *own* dream of two nights ago . . . her mother at the window, sounding so sad . . .

"But what?" Byron persisted.

"I did have one like that," Lucy murmured. "That night, after I got home from the cemetery. My mother came back to me. It was like . . . like she was trying to warn me about something."

"What'd she say?"

Lucy's voice faltered. "She said . . . that I was going to a place where . . . where she couldn't help me."

Byron gave an almost imperceptible nod. His eyes shone even darker.

"So your mother shows up with a warning. On the very night a dying girl touches you and leaves this scar on your hand. Doesn't that seem a little more than coincidence?"

"Oh God . . ."

"When I finally went to sleep that night," Byron said tightly, "I dreamed she was in a grave. I saw the storm. I saw her covered in blood . . . and I saw her reaching out."

"But . . . you didn't see who killed her?"

"No. She was talking to me . . . she wanted me to know that she was gone. And that she hadn't been alone when she died. She told me I should go to the cemetery the next morning and wait for someone. And then she said, 'Help her . . . now *you* must help the one who helped *me*.'"

Lucy didn't know how to respond. As Byron fell silent, his sorrow seemed to fill the room, yet at the same time she sensed his own defenses struggling to pull it back.

"So . . . what you're saying," she stammered, "is that *I* have these . . . these powers now. And *I'm* going to start having visions . . . and . . . and *feeling* things I don't want to feel just because I *touch* something?"

But when Byron didn't answer, Lucy's tone grew almost pleading. "Are you absolutely sure? Are you positive it was her? I mean . . . maybe she didn't even show up that night. Maybe she was never here in town. Maybe it was just some girl you didn't know, who just happened to be in the wrong place at the wrong time—"

"Lucy, stop," he said tightly.

"But it could have been, right? I mean, it *could* have been a mistake and maybe she's still alive somewhere, maybe she—"

"She's not alive."

"Then where's her body? Where's the grave? If she's really dead, you would have *found* her—you would have found *something*—"

"Lucy, stop!" His voice struck out at her, cold and final. "There are just some things you *know*, because every part of you feels it, because you have a bond with somebody that's special and unique. And she and I had that kind of bond. So . . . no. *No*. It wasn't a mistake."

He raked a hand back through his hair. His face twisted in pain.

"She's dead, Lucy. She's dead."

Lucy's heart ached at the sight of him. "You really loved her, didn't you?" she whispered.

A muscle clenched in his jaw. He turned stiffly back to the window. "Yes."

"So . . . she was your girlfriend?"

"No. Katherine was my sister."

# 21

"Your sister?" Lucy echoed. "The one who—"

She broke off, flustered, as he shot her a cold glance over his shoulder.

"Was crazy?" he finished sarcastically.

"I was going to say . . . the one who went away."

"Well, you *have* been in Pine Ridge awhile. Time enough to have heard all the gruesome stories about my family, I'm sure."

"I'm sorry." Lucy's cheeks reddened. "I haven't heard that much."

"It doesn't matter. Actually, it's not so bad, being part of the local folklore. People tend to leave you alone."

"Is that what you want? To be left alone?"

He leaned back against the wall, folding his arms across his chest, fixing her with another intense stare. "I guess that depends on who it is."

Lucy dropped her eyes. She heard him move to the fireplace and sit down upon the hearth.

"Are you sure you want to hear the rest of it?" he asked pointedly.

"Can it get any worse?" She gave him a wan smile, and he almost—but not quite—returned it.

"These . . . powers . . . forces . . . psychic abilities . . . whatever you want to call them," he began tentatively, "they run in our family. At least that's what my grandmother says. When I was little, I thought she was magic. Sometimes she could tell us things before they actually happened."

"What kinds of things?"

"Well . . . like when a certain neighbor was going to knock on our door—and then they would. Or who'd be on the other end of the phone before she even picked it up. Just simple things like that. She could tell you where to find things you'd lost . . . or that a storm was coming when there wasn't a cloud in the sky. And I never thought it was strange. It was normal to me."

Intrigued, Lucy leaned forward. "So *all* of you had psychic talents?"

"It was always so obvious with Katherine. From the time we were little, she was already having visions and seeing things nobody else could see. It was just a part of who she was. But mine was different. I was older the first time it happened. Probably around ten or so. And a woman—someone I'd never met before—had come to see my grandmother, and I remember she was so sad."

He hesitated, as though reluctant to venture too far into the past.

"I remember she was sitting at our kitchen table, waiting for Gran to come downstairs. And I sat down across from her, and suddenly she just *looked* at me. Looked me full in the face, and her eyes were so big and so desperately unhappy."

Byron's voice lowered. A poignant blend of sorrow and awe.

"I stared right back at her. Right back into her eyes. Deep, deep into that terrible sadness. And I said, 'I'm sorry about your little girl; I'm sorry she drowned.' And I remember she tried to smile at me, but she *couldn't* smile—all she could do was cry—and I felt so bad for her."

Again he paused. Then he met Lucy's gaze with a level one of his own.

"There was no way I could have known about her *or* her daughter; she didn't even live around there. Gran told me later that I'd had a glimpse of her soul."

"Eyes," Lucy murmured. "Eyes are supposed to be windows to the soul."

"Some people say so," he agreed. "I couldn't explain it then, and I don't even try anymore. But if that's true—about windows to the soul— then the daughter she'd lost was the most important feeling in her soul that day. And I had a glimpse of it."

"Is it like"—Lucy struggled for words— "looking beyond pain? Or seeing something that's even deeper than grief?"

His shoulders moved in a shrug. "It's nothing like Katherine could do—nothing that clear or sharp. No smells or sounds or things like that. It's like . . . looking through a veil. There's fog . . . mist . . . no definite features or details. Yet somehow I'm able to pull something out of it."

"Like . . . through a curtain . . . or a screen?"

"Sort of, yeah. Lucy? What is it?"

But as the memory of the confessional flashed through her mind, Lucy hurriedly shook her head. *Not now. Not yet. This isn't the right time . . .*

"Nothing," she assured him. "Tell me more about Katherine. About this gift of hers."

"A gift sometimes. But also a curse."

The edge was back in his voice, and Lucy felt a prickle of apprehension as he continued with the explanation.

"As she got older, she didn't want to use it anymore, because it scared her too much. She'd get nervous and embarrassed because she never knew when the visions would hit her—how strong they'd be, or how frightening—and most people didn't understand. Most people didn't even *try* to. All they knew was that she was different, and that sometimes she acted strange. And so some people laughed at her, and some made fun of her. And others were just plain scared."

Byron pressed both hands to his forehead . . . gently massaged his temples.

"But of course, she *couldn't* just not use it

anymore—that was impossible. It's not like a switch she could just turn on and off whenever she wanted. It was *part* of her; part of who she was. So it got to where she wouldn't even leave the house. Gran and I were the only ones she trusted; home was the only place she felt safe."

Lucy frowned, taking everything in. "But if that's true," she asked carefully, "then why did she end up leaving?"

She saw him tense . . . saw the briefest flicker of indecision over his face. She sat up straighter in her chair as her voice grew suspicious.

"There's something else," she accused him. "Something you're not telling me."

Byron stood up from the hearth. He pulled her from the rocking chair, then turned and strode purposefully to the door.

"Come with me," he said. "And I'll tell you the rest of the story."

# 22

It was a relief to get out.

Despite the coziness of the cabin, Lucy was beginning to feel claustrophobic. As if every new revelation of Byron's cast a dark, uneasy shadow over her heart and her mind.

The crisp, cold air felt wonderful. As they walked together toward the lake, the pungent fragrance of pines swirled through her head, almost making her forget, almost sweeping the doubts and fears away.

"It's so beautiful out here," Lucy murmured. She followed him to the shore, to the wooden dock stretching out over the water. A boat was tied at the end, bobbing peacefully upon the barely rippled surface, and with one smooth movement, Byron helped her down into the bow and slipped the rope free.

*Here I go again*, Lucy thought ruefully, watching the dock glide farther and farther from view—*getting myself into another dangerous situation*. And yet, out here in this pristine wilderness, surrounded by such stillness, watching Byron rhythmically work the oars, she felt a sense of peace that she hadn't felt for days.

"Don't ruin it," she said suddenly, and felt her cheeks flush as Byron gave her a curious look.

"What?"

"The mood. The minute."

He cocked his head . . . lifted an eyebrow. A playful wind tugged at his hair, streaming it back from his face. "I'll just keep rowing, then."

"So much has happened," she tried to explain, her words tumbling out in a rush. "*Too* much—too much to comprehend and understand and try to believe. And from what you're telling me—and maybe from what you're *going* to be telling me—things might be getting worse."

He didn't answer, but still, she could see the seriousness in his eyes.

"So just give me this one minute, okay? To breathe? And be away from everything that's bad? And see the world in a way that makes some sense to me."

Lucy's voice caught. She turned from him abruptly and fixed her gaze on the distant shoreline . . . on the woods and the hills and the endless blue sky above. For a long time there was only the sound of the oars dipping water . . . the music of the birds . . . the soft sigh of pine-rich breezes. Lucy shut her eyes and pretended wishes came true, and she wished this could last forever.

*But wishes never come true. At least not mine. At least not the good ones.*

As she felt the boat jar, her eyes came open. A second later the dinghy was scraping up onto a narrow stretch of beach, and Byron was out of the boat, anchoring it securely between a small shelter of trees.

"Grab those blankets under your seat," he said, reaching for her hand. "We'll go this way—I think you'll like the scenery."

"What is this? Some kind of island?"

"No, just another side of the lake. We could have driven—there's a road off that way about half a mile—but I think the boat ride's much nicer."

"How do you know about these places?" Lucy asked, as he pulled her up a steep rise and on to a stretch of level ground.

"I grew up here, remember? And I take care of a lot of these cabins off-season. And in the summer I do some maintenance work."

"What kind of maintenance work?"

"Handyman stuff, mostly."

"So that's how you had that key."

"I have all the keys."

Taking the blankets, he led her along the beach for another five minutes, then suddenly veered off again toward the shore. After maneuvering several more rocky slopes, Lucy found herself in a small, wooded cove with a breathtaking view of the lake.

"You're right, it is beautiful," she said appreciatively, gazing out across the shimmering expanse of water.

"And private." Byron shook out a blanket and spread it over the ground. "Sit down . . . wrap this other one around you. It's pretty cold out here."

Lucy did so. She watched as he sat beside her, his eyes narrowed intently on the opposite horizon. She hugged her legs to her chest and rested her chin on her knees.

"Do you believe in evil?" Byron asked.

Lucy turned to him in surprise. Somehow, surrounded by all this peaceful beauty, his question seemed almost laughable . . . and far more than ominous.

"Evil?"

"An evil that can transcend time and space? An evil so obsessive that you can't escape it, no matter how hard you try?"

Her brow creased in a frown. She drew back from him and stared harder. "You're really serious."

"You told me you thought you were being stalked the other night, when you ran from the church. Do you remember how you felt?"

"Of course I remember. I was terrified."

"Well, that's how Katherine felt all the time . . . like she was being stalked by someone. Except she couldn't outrun him. And she couldn't hide. Because he was in her visions and in her dreams."

"Byron—*what* are you talking about?"

But he wouldn't look at her, just kept staring

out across the water, at the play of light and shadow off the woods across the lake.

"They started about three years ago," he said gravely. "When she was sixteen. And they weren't like the other visions she'd had her whole life. These were like the worst kind of nightmares. Nightmares she couldn't wake up from. Nightmares she couldn't escape. Things more horrible than you could ever imagine."

With an unconscious gesture, Lucy pulled the blanket closer around her. The breeze off the beach had nothing to do with the sudden chill in her veins.

"She said it was like looking at the world through the essence of evil . . . as though *she* were inside his head, thinking out through his thoughts and seeing things through his eyes."

"Sort of"—Lucy was struggling to understand— "like a camera taking pictures?"

"Yes, capturing every gory detail as it happens."

Despite the blanket, Lucy felt even colder. "Did she tell you what these things were?"

"Never. Only that they were inhuman. So violent and hideous, she couldn't bear them anymore. Never knowing when they'd come . . . or how long they'd last. And worst of all, never being able to stop them. Just having to stand by and watch, over and over again."

"So where were these visions coming from?"

"From the mind of a monster. From someone sick and twisted, who enjoyed causing pain and watching his victims suffer."

"My God . . . so you think . . . you think this person was *real*?"

Byron's expression turned grim. "Katherine did. And she was convinced he'd keep right on killing and brutalizing people, and that he'd never get caught. Because *she* was the only one who knew about him."

"And she didn't have any idea who he was?"

"None. She never saw his face. Because she was always seeing things from *his* perspective."

Lucy could feel goose bumps along her arms. Could feel a cold, stealthy uneasiness gnawing at the back of her mind. Determinedly she tried to force it away, tried to concentrate on what Byron was saying.

"—a connection," he continued. "But why? We never knew."

"You mean, a connection between their minds? Between their thoughts? Like the bond *you* had with Katherine?"

Byron's face went rigid. "How can you even compare the two? That's—"

"No, I'm sorry, that's not what I meant," she said quickly. "I'm just trying to understand this. So Katherine could see these . . . these *atrocities* this guy was committing. *As* he was committing them?"

"Yes. *Forced* to watch him. But *helpless* to stop him."

"Then . . . was it someone she knew?"

"Impossible."

"Someone she met just one time, maybe? Someone with psychic abilities as exceptional as hers, who was somehow able to lock into her mind?"

"You mean . . . sort of like a psychic parasite?"

"Exactly."

"She hardly left the house. And this is a small community—people tend to know each other around here. I can't think of anybody who fits into an evil mode like this one. And believe me . . . I've tried."

"But you said she sensed things—*saw* things—by touching. So maybe she bumped into him in a crowd . . . I mean, he could have just been passing through town, or visiting somebody here. Maybe he dropped something . . . or . . . or accidentally left something of his behind. And Katherine just happened to pick it up."

Byron sounded weary. "I've thought of that, too. And I guess it *is* possible . . . except I think she'd only have felt a connection to it when it was in her hands. Just when she touched it. *Not* on and on for three years."

"But maybe she kept it. Maybe she found something, and took it home with her and didn't realize."

"She'd have realized, Lucy, believe me."

Lucy went silent. She watched as he leaned back on the ground, propping himself on his elbows. He stared far out at the opposite bank, and his gaze narrowed, hard as steel.

"Katherine was such a gentle person. Probably the only truly good person I've ever known in my life. And that's what made it so much worse. The way she suffered . . . her fear and her pain . . . There were times she really thought she was losing her mind. And sometimes I think . . ." His voice faltered . . . softened. "I think maybe . . . finally . . . in a way . . ."

A shadow seemed to cross his face. After a moment of uncertain silence, Lucy gently touched his shoulder.

"Wasn't there anyone she could talk to? Someone who could help her?"

"And who would that have been? How do you explain something like that—especially in a town like this? Hell, everybody here *already* thought she was crazy."

"But maybe someone who has experience in—"

"Ssh!" Jerking upright, Byron grabbed her shoulder. "Did you hear something?"

Lucy's heart took a dive to her stomach. As she slowly followed the direction of his gaze, she listened hard through the quiet.

Wind sighing through trees . . . water lapping gently at the shore . . . her own pulse pounding in her ears . . .

"What?" she mouthed silently. "What is it?"

But she could feel his grip relaxing now . . . his body easing back down beside her. His hand slid away from her arm, though his expression remained wary.

"What?" she asked aloud, but Byron only frowned and turned his attention back to the view.

"Nothing. Just jumpy, I guess."

Lucy glanced nervously over her shoulder. Strange . . . she hadn't really heard anything, yet she could feel a tiny sliver of dread at the back of her neck.

"It's okay," Byron reassured her again. "This is one of my secret places . . . and nobody's around here this time of year anyway."

Lucy wasn't entirely convinced. She picked up a broken twig and nervously began scratching circles in the dirt.

"What about your grandmother?" she asked then. "Does she know about Katherine?"

His mouth twisted in a rueful smile. "There's not much Gran doesn't know. But I haven't told her, if that's what you mean."

"So . . . do you think *she* believes Katherine's dead?"

Byron fixed her with a calm stare. "When Katherine left home a year ago—that was before

Gran had her stroke—Gran told me I'd never see Katherine alive again. I didn't want to believe that, of course. I should have known better. Maybe if I'd tried harder to stop Katherine from going . . . or maybe if I'd gone with her, maybe she'd still be alive now. That's why you have to listen to me—maybe we can stop it this time—before you get hurt—"

"Before *I* get hurt?" Lucy shrank back in dismay. "What do you mean—"

"Because maybe he hasn't realized it yet—"

"Byron—"

"—hasn't realized yet who you are—"

"Stop it! You're scaring me!"

"You *should* be scared, Lucy—you *need* to be scared! It might be the only thing that keeps you alive if—"

He broke off abruptly, his body tensing, his glance shooting once more toward the trees. As Lucy followed the direction of his focus, she felt that fine prickle of fear again, though now it was creeping down the length of her arms.

Very slowly Byron got to his feet. As Lucy started to follow, he shook his head at her and held a finger to his lips.

"No," he whispered. "Wait here."

"Where are you going?" Thoroughly alarmed now, Lucy watched him disappear into the woods. She stood there, heart pounding, listening to the faint rustle of branches as Byron moved away from her. But even that sound faded within minutes.

All that remained was silence.

*Dangerous silence.*

Should she call his name? Ignore what he'd told her and go after him? Lucy didn't know what to do. With the lake on one side and the woods on all others, this spot that had seemed so idyllic just five minutes before, now seemed more like a . . .

*Trap.*

*That's it. I'm going.*

Lucy started toward the trees, toward the exact spot where Byron had gone in. Surely he couldn't be that far ahead of her—it should be easy to catch up. But what if she got lost? She'd be of no use to him then, and someone had to be able to go for help.

She wished she had a weapon. Quickly her eyes scanned the shore, coming to rest on a large branch dangling over the water. With some effort, she managed to wrestle it loose; she could use it as a club if she had to.

"*Lucy!*"

Lucy froze. She hadn't imagined it, had she? That voice calling through the trees . . .

"Byron?" she yelled back.

It had sounded so faint, that call—distant and muffled. *Oh God, maybe he really is hurt.* Why had he just gone off like that, anyway—what a stupid thing to do!

Lucy squinted off through the shifting shadows of the forest. Cupping her hands around her mouth, she shouted as loud as she could. "By-ron!"

No answer.

*I* didn't *imagine it—I'm* sure *I* didn't imagine it!

Yet at the same time the hairs lifted at the back of her neck, and her nerves went taut as wires. *Just like I didn't imagine that voice in the confessional, that voice behind the tent at the fair . . .*

She wished now that she'd told Byron about that voice—*why* hadn't she told Byron about it?

"Byron!" she called frantically. "Byron, where *are* you?"

The wind blew a long cold breeze in off the lake.

It wrapped around her like a damp caress.

"Lucy!" the voice seemed to echo, ghostly through the hills. "Please, Lucy! I need you!"

"Oh, God . . . oh God . . ." She knew then that something *must* have happened to him—something bad—something terrible—and it was all she could do to hold her panic in check.

"I'm coming!" Lucy shouted.

And ran headlong into the woods.

# 23

"Byron! Where are you?"

But she hadn't heard him call in several minutes now, and she knew she'd be hopelessly lost if she went much farther.

Frightened and frustrated, Lucy stopped and yelled one more time. "Byron! *Please!* Answer me!"

Even the breeze seemed to have stopped. Even the trees seemed to hold their breath around her.

Maybe he'd been injured so badly that he'd lost consciousness by now. Mauled by some animal. Lying broken at the bottom of some ravine. Slowly and steadily bleeding to death. *Oh God, what should I do?* If she ended up lost in these dark woods, it wouldn't do *either* of them any good.

Instinctively, Lucy turned and raced back to the beach. Had there been a radio in the boat? A cell phone? She didn't remember seeing any, but she hadn't been paying much attention. As she broke through the trees, she suddenly halted in her tracks and stared in shock at the lake.

A small boat was floating some distance from the shore.

An empty boat.

*Our boat?*

"*No!*"

Lucy couldn't believe it. A thousand menacing scenarios rushed through her head, muddling into a numbing darkness. Fearfully she spun around and peered off into the forest.

"*Byron!*"

Her shout echoed back to her, mocking.

She had to think . . . think what to do. Try to find help—but where? She didn't have a clue where to go—and what if Bryon roused again and called for her? Still, he was familiar with this place . . . perhaps even now he was on his way to safety . . .

*The road!*

Lucy suddenly remembered—hadn't Byron mentioned a road when they'd first gotten out of the boat? A road about half a mile from here?

Praying she could find her way back to the cove, Lucy tried to retrace the route they'd taken earlier. She'd noticed a pathway, a narrow trail leading back from the beach and angling off through the woods. As she finally reached the place where they'd originally docked, Lucy could see the path clearly, and she took it without hesitation.

The trail wound mostly uphill, and though she'd been chilly when she first started out she soon grew sweaty and out of breath. She was thankful she'd worn her sneakers. More than once she was forced to scale fallen logs and sharp boulders that blocked the rugged terrain.

She wasn't sure when she began to be aware of the quiet. It seemed to slip up on her gradually, like shadows stalking through underbrush. As she stopped to listen, Lucy realized that the birds had stopped singing, that there wasn't a breath of wind.

The forest filled with an eerie silence.

*Just like it felt back there when I was looking for Byron . . .*

Her heart fluttered beneath her jacket. She forced herself to keep walking, to keep her thoughts carefully focused on the emergency at hand. Find help. Find Byron. She couldn't let herself think of anything beyond that. She just hoped he wasn't hurt—

*"Maybe we can stop it this time—before you get hurt—"*

Lucy's eyes widened as his words sprang unexpectedly into her mind. *No. No. I won't think about that; I refuse to think about that . . .*

*"Because maybe he hasn't realized it yet—hasn't realized yet who you are—"*

And Byron had started to tell her something, something important, had been trying to warn her about something, when the sound had come, when he'd looked so startled and so wary, when he'd gone into the woods and never come out again . . .

*"You should be scared, Lucy—you need to be scared! It might be the only thing that keeps you alive if—"*

Lucy broke into a run.

And the silence was so loud, so dangerous, threatening her from every side, silence like shadows, silence like stalkers . . .

*No—no—it's just my imagination—*

Silence like evil . . .

*No!*

Silence like death—

Her feet slid off into nothingness; her body hurtled down through an endless black void . . .

She didn't even have time to scream.

Just fell farther and farther . . . down and down . . . into the silence . . .

And finally lay still.

# 24

She was so beautiful.

Beautiful in this brief spell of sleep . . . lost in her dreamless drifting . . .

*Is this what peace looks like?* he wondered.

The way *she'd* looked that night at her window, and the way she'd looked at the Festival . . . her face tilted, smiling, bathed in the glow of the lights, just so . . .

And now . . . as she lay here on her back, unconscious from falling, sprawled before him in innocent slumber . . .

He could do anything he wanted to her at this very moment, anything he pleased, for she'd be helpless and completely unaware . . .

But time enough for that later.

Right now all he wanted to do was look at her.

At her hair spread around her head like a halo, her lashes soft against her cheeks. Her fingers curled in upon her palms, like flower petals unopened, and her arms wide in an empty embrace, half buried beneath the leaves that had cushioned her fall.

She was still wearing red.

He loved her even more when she wore red.

It seared into his soul, this brand-new image, like the pink of that very first night . . . like the blue of the Festival . . . and oh, how he'd loved the deep bloodred of her panic and terror at the church just this morning . . .

He'd carried those sights of her, those smells of her, deep in his heart through every single hour since then.

Like a seductive dream, both sleeping and waking.

It was sheer luck that he'd tasted her, as well . . .

He'd picked up the apple she'd dropped at the fair, and she'd never suspected, never stopped to look back, never even realized he was near. And ah, how it tasted just the way he'd imagined . . . the blood from her lip still fresh on the fruit . . . so luscious, so sweet, with its red candy coating.

He'd savored the juice of it inside his mouth, and then he'd lured her to a dark, hidden place.

She'd caught his scent, and she'd come to him . . .

He *loved* how she loved the scent of him.

The way he *always* smelled after he killed.

For blood, as he'd come to learn through the years, was a very personal thing.

It mingled with one's own essence . . . and tempted . . . like expensive cologne or perfume.

She'd followed him there, and she'd found him there, and when he'd sucked the blood from her lip, her heart had beat wildly, as frantically as his own . . .

And after that—*especially* after that—he vowed that *nothing* would stop him from having her.

Only . . . not now.

Not now.

Now he would simply watch and admire . . .

For this was the sweetest torment of all.

The ache of her loneliness . . . the pain of her grief . . .

He *fed* off emotions such as these, they *called* to him like shining beacons in pitch-black rooms.

They made him dizzy with longing, and they made him want to possess her totally.

Soon, he told himself. *Soon . . .*

He had to be patient with this one.

Not arouse suspicion . . . gain her trust. That was how these things were done . . . slow and methodical . . . and he was nothing if not methodical.

It was a fine art he'd perfected through these many years—that when he desired something, he'd do *anything* to get it.

Say anything . . . *be* anything . . . no matter how deceitful, no matter how ruthless.

It was his nature.

And he could wait for however long it took.

*No need to hurry*, he reminded himself.

No need whatsoever to rush.

After all . . . he had eternity on his side.

# 25

"*Lu-cy . . .*"

"Mom?" Lucy mumbled.

She always sounded like that when she'd locked herself out of the apartment, standing down on the street corner, yelling up at Lucy's bedroom window . . .

"*Lu-cy . . .*"

It was ridiculous; she was always telling Mom how ridiculous it was, a grown woman forgetting her keys all the time, leaving them at work or at the grocery store or on the kitchen table: *I mean, one of these days I'm not going to be here, I won't be here to let you in, and then what are you going to do?*

"Lucy!"

"Hang on, I'm coming . . . I'm . . ."

Cobwebs drifted through her mind, but they

were getting thinner now, almost transparent, and there was light coming through . . .

"Coming . . ." she murmured.

Lucy sat up so quickly that the world spun around her and the cobwebs burst like bubbles.

She didn't realize at first what had happened.

Not until she shook herself out of the leaves and squinted up at the walls of the ravine and saw a shadowy blur of trees and sky high above her.

*I was running just a minute ago . . . how'd I get down here?*

She ached all over. Her clothes were twisted around her, and she was covered with dirt. *This is starting to feel normal*, she thought disgustedly, stretching out her arms and then her legs. At least nothing seemed to be broken or sprained. *So far, so good . . .*

*Byron!*

It all came back to her then—why she was out here in the middle of the woods, what must have happened. She should have been paying attention, watched where she was going—now what was she going to do? If Byron were still out there somewhere, wounded or even dying, she'd never get help back to him in time. Gazing up at the steep incline, she wasn't even sure she could help *herself*.

"Damnit," Lucy muttered, fighting down panic. "*Damnit!*" Her body winced with pain as she tried to stand up. She hobbled over to one side of the gorge, then suddenly noticed the outline of a head hanging over the ledge above her.

"Lucy!" Even from down here, she could hear Byron's sigh of relief. "Are you okay?"

"Am I okay?" her voice shot back to him, dangerously close to tears. "Do I *look* okay? My *God*, Byron—where have you *been?*"

"What are you doing down there?"

"Trying to save you!"

He leaned out farther over the edge. Lucy heard the sarcasm in his voice. "And a fine job you're doing, too."

"Get me out of here! You scared me to death!"

"I'll be right down."

Lucy sagged back against the wall of the escarpment, wiping furiously at her eyes. By the time Byron finally worked his way down beside her, her nerves were raw.

"I thought you were dead!" she exploded. "Where *were* you? Why didn't you answer me?"

Byron regarded her solemnly. "I could ask you the same question."

"What are you talking about? *I'm* not the one who was lost!"

"Then who have I been looking for? I heard you calling for help, but I couldn't find you anywhere."

"*I'm* not the one who called for help—*you're* the one who called for help! *You're* the one who disappeared!" Lucy was trembling now, with anger and relief. "You're the one who went off and *left* me! I called and called, and the boat floated away!"

Byron's eyes narrowed. "You mean, *you* didn't take the boat?"

"Why would I do that? It was out in the middle of the lake! Then I tried to find a road— so I could get someone to look for you! And then—"

"Lucy," he interrupted, taking her shoulders, giving her a gentle shake. "Lucy, listen to me, I'm telling you the truth. I heard your voice, but it was so deep in the woods—and you kept saying my name, calling for help. You sounded like you were crying, like you'd been hurt. But I looked and looked, and I couldn't find you. I've been searching for three hours!"

Lucy stared back at him, calmer now, but bewildered. "But . . . I heard *you*, too—and I thought *you* were hurt—"

"You heard *me*? When?"

"Right after you went into the woods! I was so scared and—" She broke off abruptly at the expression on his face. "What? What is it?"

"I didn't call you, Lucy. I *never* called you. I was . . ."

"*What?*"

"I was afraid for you." For a second he seemed almost angry. He clenched his jaw, and something dark flickered far back in his eyes. "I didn't want anyone to know you were here. So I didn't call you."

Lucy hadn't realized she was trembling again. Taking her arm, Byron sat her on the ground and knelt beside her.

"Then who did?" Lucy whispered. "Who did?"

Byron shook his head, his gaze lowered. Then

finally he said, "I was trying to tell you when I heard something in the woods."

"What's going on, Byron? I don't under-stand."

The lines of his face went hard. "The truth is, I brought you here to warn you."

"To . . . warn me? Why? About what?"

"Lucy, the night Katherine left home, she woke me up and told me she couldn't stand to see Gran and me hurting for her anymore. And that she was going to *go* wherever she had to, and *do* whatever she had to, to learn the truth about those evil visions. She swore that no matter what it took, she'd put them to rest, once and for all."

"So you think she actually tried to find that evil person who was connecting to her thoughts?"

"I think she *did* find him. And I think he killed her."

Lucy watched the carefully controlled rage in his expression . . . the muscle working tightly in his cheek.

"Katherine was wearing that green necklace when she went away. It was a present I'd given her years before, and she never took it off. But yesterday morning I found it in the cemetery, so I knew—*I knew then for certain*—that she was dead. She'd never have taken it off otherwise. Never."

"So you think it came off in the struggle?"

"I think she *took* it off *because* of the struggle. To leave a clue behind . . . and a warning."

He paused a second, chewing thoughtfully on his lower lip. Then he turned to Lucy with a grave frown.

"I think Katherine's murderer touched that necklace while she was fighting for her life. And I think she left it there on purpose *because* he'd touched it, and I think she passed her power on to you, so *someone* would know who killed her."

Lucy went pale. "So you're saying . . . that when I held the necklace, I was actually seeing her . . . her death?"

Without another word she jumped up and started pacing.

"Lucy!"

"No, I don't *want* this—I don't want any *part* of this—I didn't *ask* for this—I—"

"You don't have a choice." Byron was on his feet again, beside her in an instant. "You *are* part of it now, whether you like it or not. There's nothing you can do but accept it."

"And anyway, when I *did* hold the necklace, I didn't see anyone!" Lucy babbled, as though she hadn't heard a single word Bryon said. "I didn't see the face of any killer! I just felt wind and there were eyes and hands and blood and . . . and . . ."

He reached out for her and held her at arms length, forcing her to look at him. "I told you, sometimes it doesn't happen all at once. The next time you touch it, you might see something else, something more—"

"There won't *be* a next time! I'm *not* going to hold that necklace! I'm not going to touch *anything*!" Angrily, Lucy broke free from his grasp. "You don't even know if the guy in Katherine's visions and the guy who killed her are the same person! You don't even know for sure if the guy in her visions was real! I mean, maybe she truly was . . . was . . . sick, and she couldn't help it. I'm sorry, but it *is* possible— people can be sick—"

"Like my mother." Byron's tone was frosty. "I'm assuming that's who you mean?"

"I . . ." Lucy looked at him helplessly. Everything was wrong, everything was falling in on her, the *world* was falling in on her, and she was all alone, and she couldn't get away. "I didn't mean—"

"I want to show you something," Byron said.

Lucy watched him reach into his pocket and pull out a crumpled piece of paper, ragged and soiled around the edges, as though it had been folded and unfolded, read and reread many times.

"This is the last message I got from Katherine. She asks me to meet her at the church. She says she needs to talk to me about something important. And then she ends it with this."

He thrust it out to Lucy. Reluctantly she looked down at the note, where two words had been hastily scrawled at the bottom of the page.

*HE LIVES*

# 26

A feeling of numbness crept over her.

She handed the paper back.

"I'm going now, Byron. I'm going to climb out of here and find the road and go home. Even if I have to walk all the way back to town."

"Lucy—"

"No. Don't talk to me. I just want to go."

Somehow she made it up the embankment. As she reached the top, she was surprised to see cuts and scrapes all over her hands, and rips in the knees of her jeans. Dusting herself off as best she could, Lucy started walking. From somewhere behind her, she was vaguely aware that Byron was following. But it wasn't till he yelled after her that she stopped.

"But you can't ignore it, can you? Because things have been happening to you, haven't they? Other things besides the necklace? Things you can't explain? And they're scaring you, aren't they? They're scaring you to death!"

Lucy spun around, enraged. "Leave me alone! You don't know anything!"

"Then tell me! Why don't you tell me? I want to help!"

"How can you help?" Tears brimmed in her eyes and she fought to keep her voice steady. "You couldn't even help Katherine! You couldn't even keep her from dying, could you?"

She saw his face, the anger and grief in his tortured expression. "Don't you think I know that? Don't you think I've been tormented by that? Do you have any idea how horrible it was, watching her go through that? Watching somebody you love suffer like she did, with no explanations and no help?"

His voice quivered with rage. His dark eyes flashed with helpless frustration.

"And the same thing will happen to you. You'll try to warn people, but they won't believe you. You'll try to save people, but you'll fail. You'll see tragedies that you won't be able to prevent, and you'll feel every single human grief and suffering and sorrow like a knife thrust deep in your heart. I saw what it did to her. Day by day, and tragedy by tragedy, it wore her down, it poisoned her mind. I *know* in my heart she was happy to die in the end . . . she was *glad* to be free from that *gift* of hers."

Lucy stood there, unable to move, watching the anguish pour out of him. It was like watching a dam break in slow motion, and then, finally, wondering how it had ever held up for so long.

"Oh, God, Byron," Lucy whispered. "I'm so sorry."

She moved toward him at last. She reached out and gently touched his cheek, and for a brief moment, the walls remained down and unguarded.

"All right," she murmured. "I'll tell you everything."

With almost numb detachment, Lucy recounted every strange and frightening event of the past few days. They sat together on a low outcrop of rocks, facing each other while she admitted her doubts to him, questioned her reasoning and wild imagination, allowed for the possibility of coincidence.

Byron listened attentively . . . but it wasn't until she'd finished that he finally allowed himself to comment.

"You can't *really* believe you imagined all that." His tone was slightly incredulous. "You *can't* believe those are coincidences. And especially after what just happened now in the woods."

Lucy let out a weary sigh. "I don't know what I think anymore."

For an endless moment silence settled between them. Then Byron said quietly, "Katherine warned you not to tell anyone, didn't she? Because your life could be in danger."

"Yes." Reluctantly Lucy nodded. "So . . . why? Because she was afraid he'd kill me, too?"

"What did he say in the confessional? When you asked him who he was?"

She shuddered, merely thinking about it. "He told me he was my salvation."

Byron looked thoughtful. He ran his fingers slowly along his chin. "You said he wasn't there when you found Katherine. He may not even realize yet that she passed her powers on to you. In fact . . . he might not even know you were there at all."

"If that's true, then why is he suddenly so interested in me?"

"I'm not sure. But I think if we can figure out what his connection was to *Katherine*, that might help us figure out what his connection is to you."

Lucy's shoulders sagged. Lowering her head, she covered her face with her hands and groaned. "And what if we don't? What if we never do?"

"He could have been here today," Byron speculated, dodging her question. "Tricking us into getting separated. Untying the boat. Hoping you'd be alone . . ."

"So what you're telling me is, he could be anywhere. He could be anyone. Watching me. All the time."

"That's why we have to go back and get the necklace. I think we need to start there. It'll give us a clue to who killed Katherine. And why."

"I just hope it's still there at the church," Lucy said glumly.

"You said some priest had it?"

She nodded. "Matt. Father Matt."

"And what'd he do with it?"

"He just said he was going to put it back where he found it—by the altar. In case whoever dropped it came back for it. But if you want to talk to him, I think he's going to be there all day, going through storage closets and stuff."

Byron hesitated. "I don't think we should go back till he leaves."

"Why not? Why would he think anything about it?"

"You're the one who heard voices in the confessional. You tell me." Then, at Lucy's distressed look, he said quickly, "Look, I just think the less people who know about any of this, the better. Doesn't that make sense?"

"You're right," she agreed. "And by the way, how did you get into the church this morning, if Father Matt wasn't there yet?"

Bryon raised an eyebrow. "Gran used to be the cleaning lady at the church. I have a key."

"So you weren't lying. You *do* have all the keys. To just about everything."

She thought he almost smiled at that. He stood and pulled her to her feet.

"Do you really think the necklace is going to help me?" As Lucy gazed up into his face, her eyes were almost pleading.

Byron stared down at her, a faint frown creasing his brow. Then, with wary tenderness, he lifted his hand and lightly touched her cheek.

"Only if we find it before the killer does."

# 27

Luckily, they didn't have far to walk.

As they finally came out on the other side of the woods, Byron recognized the driver of a passing pickup truck and flagged him down for a ride.

"Well, Byron, what brings you up today?" The old man greeted Byron with a grin.

"Just checking some cabins, Ray." Byron introduced Lucy, then added, "Do you think you could help me out? I borrowed Mac's boat, and it came untied back there at the cove. I don't have time to look for it 'cause I need to get Lucy back to town."

Ray gave them a wink. "Don't you worry. I'll tow it back, and nobody'll ever know it was gone."

"Thanks, I appreciate it."

As they neared the cabin where Lucy had

left the car, Byron casually asked if anyone had noticed any suspicious activity around the area.

"Haven't seen anything like that," Ray said anxiously. "Why? Something wrong?"

Byron's answer was casual and calculated. "Just wondering. It looks like someone might have tried to break into the Millers' place."

"Well, I'll sure keep a lookout," Ray promised. "If I see any strangers, I'll be sure and report them right away."

Squeezed tightly together in the front seat, Lucy gave Byron a grateful smile. When Ray let them out at the cabin, they waited till he was out of sight, then locked up and headed back into town.

"How about I pick you up around seven?" Byron asked her. "The church should be locked up again by then."

"I think we should meet somewhere," Lucy suggested instead. "Angela's way too nosy, and Irene's been in a horrible mood. I'd rather not borrow more trouble."

Byron agreed. "What about the Festival, then?"

"Well . . . I'm pretty sure Angela will want to go back. But she's supposed to be grounded, so I'll have to see if we can sneak out again."

"Can you lose her once you get there?"

"No problem. The less she has to be with me, the more she likes it. Besides, I think she's been hanging out with some guy there she doesn't want her mom to know about."

"Perfect. I'll meet you at the carousel."

After letting Byron out at his house, Lucy went on to the car wash. She hadn't realized how exhausted she was, but now, with the turbulent morning behind her, she could feel all her emotions letting down at last. She drove through the car wash, relishing the blasts of water and churning brushes all around her, feeling in some strange way almost as cleansed as the Corvette.

It gave her time to collect her thoughts. Angela would demand an explanation when she got back; that much she could count on. She told herself she had to act normally, think clearly, come up with some logical excuses for being so late. She remembered the few times Irene had suggested that Lucy go shopping for new clothes, mentioning stores where she could use Irene's accounts.

*Yes. Good cover.* Glancing down at her stained jeans and jacket, Lucy thought how funny that was. On a whim, she stopped at the same fast-food restaurant she'd stopped at that morning, and slipped into the women's restroom. Using bunches of paper towels, she did her best at a hasty cleanup, then ran a comb through her hair. *Fine. That'll work.*

Driving home, her thoughts kept wandering, even though she tried to keep them in check. Thinking too much was dangerous to her now, she decided—the slightest little thing might send her over the edge. How could a day start off so innocently, then turn so deadly? How could your life change completely in a matter of seconds? And how could she and Katherine—a girl she'd never met and would never even know—become so tragically intertwined?

*So much for fate,* Lucy thought wearily.

How strange it was, the way events wove themselves together, pulling innocent people into the middle of darkness, into the middle of bad surprises. If only she hadn't gone for a walk the other night, none of this would have happened. *If only Mom hadn't died, I wouldn't be here in the first place. If only . . . if only . . .*

No use going there, she told herself sternly. There was nothing she could do about any of it till tonight. *Except drive yourself crazy with worrying.*

She heard the battle before she was even halfway in the back door. Irene and Angela in the kitchen, voices raised at fever pitch. Angela's furious tears, and Irene's unyielding authority.

"You were *seen* there last night, Angela!" Irene was livid. "I *told* you you were grounded, and you *deliberately* disobeyed me!"

"It wasn't my fault!" Angela whined.

"Did you actually think it wouldn't get back to me?" Irene countered. "In this town where I know so many people? I can't trust you for a minute, can I? But I *told* you what would happen, and now you have to accept the consequences. No car. Period. Not to school, not anywhere. And your credit cards—as of right now—are canceled."

"You can't do that!"

"I just did."

"I'm not giving them to you!"

"Angela, it doesn't matter. I have all the numbers right here in my briefcase, and it's as good as done. Now go upstairs."

"Daddy would *never* have treated me this way!"

"Well, he's not here. And if he *had* treated you a little more this way, you wouldn't be so selfish and self-indulgent."

"I'll run away!"

"Oh, Angela, don't be ridiculous. You couldn't survive for one night without all the comforts of home. Just once I'd like to be able to walk out this door and leave this house without having to go through all these theatrics."

"I swear I will! I'll run away where you'll never find me—"

"It was my fault," Lucy announced.

Irene and Angela both turned in surprise. Lucy took a deep breath and came boldly into the room.

"It was my fault," she said again. She could see Irene's mask of a face, her look of perpetual disapproval.

"Lucy?" Irene raised one suspicious eyebrow.

"I wanted to go to the Festival last night, and I didn't know how to get there." Lucy squared her shoulders. "And you know how horrible I am at directions. And Angela *told* me she was grounded, but . . . but I begged her."

Irene wasn't to be swayed. "That's no excuse. Angela should have known better."

"But it was my fault," Lucy insisted again. "Angela didn't even stay. She dropped me off there, and then she came back to pick me up later. And . . . I forgot where we were supposed to meet, so she had to come and look for me."

Irene gave an impassive nod. "I see."

Lucy glanced at Angela. Angela's expression was stubborn and defiant. Irene looked at one girl, and then at the other.

Finally she said, "Lucy, I also expect *you* to abide by house rules."

"I know." Lucy nodded contritely. "I'm sorry."

"Both of you go upstairs."

"What about my credit cards?" Angela demanded.

"I told you," Irene said. "Canceled."

With a cry of rage, Angela stomped up to her room. As Lucy stood by uncertainly, Irene gathered her overnight bag, briefcase, her purse and her coat.

"I've left the hotel number by the phone. I should be home early tomorrow afternoon."

Lucy nodded. As Irene passed through the door, she gave Lucy a frosty glare.

"That was very noble of you, Lucy. It's admirable of you to want to protect your cousin . . . but in the future, I won't tolerate lying. Even if you *are* trying to be noble."

Lucy made a hasty exit, bracing herself against the blast of Angela's music that shook her bedroom walls. After a while she heard Irene leaving and the music promptly shutting off.

She lay down across the bed and buried her face in her arms. She wanted to sleep. She wanted to sleep and sleep and just forget . . .

She drifted. She heard the kitchen door open and shut several times, Angela going up and down the stairs, but she was too tired to wonder about it. She wondered instead how she could rearrange the evening now, how she'd manage to get out of the house. Irene had not only issued orders, she'd confiscated Angela's car keys. It would be tricky now, getting back to the Festival.

She shouldn't have worried.

"Come on!" Angela announced several hours later, bursting through the door. Lucy nearly jumped out of her skin.

"What do you think you're doing?" she demanded.

"What do *you* think? Going to the Festival!"

"Angela, are you insane? After that major blowup with Irene?"

"Do I look like I care?"

"If someone saw you there *last* night, they're bound to see you again tonight! Irene's probably hired spies! She'll be furious!"

"Trust me . . ." Angela said mysteriously. "Irene will never know."

"Angela, what—"

"Don't ask questions. Just get in the car."

"But the keys—"

With a Cheshire cat grin, she dangled an extra set between her fingers. "Do I look that stupid to you?"

"Angela—"

"Do you wanna go or *not*?"

Lucy thought about how much trouble they'd be in. And then she thought about the necklace and all that was at stake.

And then she nodded and grabbed her jacket. "Yes," she said. "I definitely want to go."

# 28

Despite Lucy's reluctance—and the fact that Irene had confiscated her license, as well—Angela insisted on driving. Lucy spent the whole ride slumped down in the seat, as though by making herself invisible, no police would dare to stop their car. Unfortunately, Angela wasn't in such a law-abiding mode—she couldn't wait to do every single reckless thing she could think of, now that Irene had left town.

"I have a bad feeling about tonight," Lucy said, but Angela just laughed.

"Trust me. I will *not* get grounded for this."

"Angela, you've lost your mind. You truly have."

"I will *not* get grounded or punished in any way, shape, or form, thank you very much."

"If you say so."

"Come on, Lucy—just have a little faith."

Lucy breathed a sigh of relief when they arrived at the Festival. As the two of them walked through the gates, she didn't even have to come up with an excuse. Angela flipped her a wave and headed straight into the crowd.

"Meet you same time same place," Lucy said.

Angela beamed at her. "Hey! Don't count on it!"

"Angela?" Lucy shouted, but the girl just ignored her. "Angela!"

*What is she up to?* Lucy didn't have time to worry about it, though. Byron was waiting for her, as promised, right by the carousel.

"Ready?" he asked.

"As I'll ever be."

Taking her arm, he steered her toward the exit. Lucy couldn't help noticing some of the looks they got on their way—girls eyeing them with a mixture of curiosity and blatant envy. When she was certain he wasn't looking, she stole a look up at Byron's face—the handsomely chiseled features set off by that guarded, mysterious stare. Now she found herself wondering if anyone else really understood that expression, the way she'd come to know it today. She doubted if he'd ever shown such vulnerability before; she doubted he'd ever be so willing again.

Still, seeing the wistful looks cast in their direction she couldn't help but get a warm feeling inside. She was only human, after all. *Nothing like calling attention to yourself, Lucy.* Her appearance with Byron Wetherly would be all over school by homeroom Monday morning.

The world lay shrouded in black. There were no stars tonight, only a bloodred moon, full and round. As they drove through town to the old church, Lucy watched it, fascinated, as it seemed to follow them through the pale tattered clouds.

"Full moon," Byron said, noting the focus of her stare. "No wonder things have been so strange around here."

Lucy suppressed a little shiver. "I've never seen the moon that color before—it's creepy."

He glanced at her sideways, but said nothing.

The church looked ominous as ever when they pulled up and parked. Byron cut the headlights, and they sat there a moment, listening to the muffled sounds of the night. The sky flowed like thick oil overhead . . . a light mist swirled through the graveyard.

"Nice horror movie," Byron commented dryly.

Lucy nodded. It was the only church she'd ever seen that made her feel so unsettled. And she didn't feel any *less* unsettled once they'd gone inside.

They stood side by side, their eyes readjusting to an almost stygian darkness. Byron took a flashlight from his jacket pocket and quietly flicked it on. They seemed to be alone. Their footfalls echoed hollowly as they walked up the aisle, and Lucy could hear the faint scurryings of mice darting beneath the pews. As they neared the altar, a fiendish howl suddenly rose up, disembodied, from the gloom. It echoed back from the damp stone walls . . . wafted through the shadows . . . shivered down along her spine.

Instinctively she grabbed for Byron's arm.

Then let out a nervous laugh.

"Cats," she mumbled. "Matt said they keep cats in here. For rodent control."

Even Byron seemed momentarily unnerved by the spectral howl. As a large black cat slipped around the end of the altar, he shone his flashlight on it, causing it to freeze instantly. It arched its back and hissed, then crouched down again and slunk away.

"Not very friendly," Byron murmured, putting one hand on her back, guiding her gently forward.

"Well, he sure didn't seem to like *you* much."

Byron ignored the remark. "Do you see it?" he asked her, squinting through the blackness.

Lucy, too, strained her eyes, running her hands over the dusty altar cloth. "No. But he said he'd leave it right here."

"Maybe he forgot."

Lucy sighed. "Then we'll never find it—he could have put it anywhere. He could have taken it with him, for that matter."

She turned to see Byron standing by the confessionals, and her heart gave a fearful twist.

"Is this where it happened?" he asked softly. "Where you saw . . . well . . . whoever he was you saw?"

Lucy nodded reluctantly. As if merely conjuring the memory might bring it back again in all its terror.

"He must have been in here already," Byron mused. "Before you showed up. From where I was sitting, I would have seen him go in."

"He could have come through some other way though. Matt mentioned some cellars. In these old places, there could be lots of entrances, right? Even secret ones."

"Possibly."

Byron's voice echoed, empty and toneless. Even the shadows seemed to slither away from it, skulking along the walls and ceiling, worse than any cats. She watched uneasily as he opened one of the confessional doors. As he shone the light in and skimmed it over the dark, cramped space.

"And when you came out from here . . . it was just the priest," he murmured.

Lucy wished they could talk about something else. "But it couldn't have been him," she said, almost defensively.

He lifted an eyebrow. "I didn't say it was."

He opened the priest's compartment, following the same slow ritual with his flashlight. He opened the door on the opposite side.

All of them, empty.

"Byron," Lucy said suddenly, "let's go."

He turned to her in wary surprise. "What's wrong?"

"I . . . I don't know. I just . . ."

Her voice trailed away. She cast a nervous look around them, down the center aisle, the intersecting pews, the dirty linen altar cloth.

"Please," she whispered. Was it getting colder in here? Just like the time before . . . just like the last time when she'd heard the whisper . . . followed the voice . . . seen that malevolent shadow behind the screen . . .

"Byron . . ."

And she could see *him* looking now, too, trying to follow the direction of her eyes, trying to see what was wrong. And somehow she knew what would come next . . . she was *expecting* it—was *ready* for it—and yes, she realized with a shock, *longing* for it, as well, like the scent of a favorite flower or the warmth of a favorite memory that transported the spirit back to sweeter times . . .

Without another word she turned and ran for the doors.

"Lucy! Wait!"

She could hear Byron shouting at her, but she didn't stop. She put her hands against the doors and pushed, but they wouldn't open.

"Oh, God!"

She struggled against them, pushing, pushing, and she could see the crazy arc of the flashlight sweeping the ceiling, over the faces of the saints, the broken shards of agonies and ecstasies and long-forgotten prayers . . .

"Lucy—for God's sake—"

With one last effort, her body fell against them, and the doors burst wide and welcomed the night in.

Screaming, Lucy toppled right into a strong pair of arms.

And a very shocked expression.

Shielding himself from her flailing limbs, Matt tried to steady Lucy and keep his balance at the same time. The next thing she knew, Byron had ahold of her, both his arms around her, restraining her and pulling her back.

"Lucy—what is *wrong* with you?"

She stopped struggling. She stared at Matt, who was staring back at her—tousled hair, easy grin, only now the grimy jeans and sweatshirt had been replaced with black pants, black shirt, and a priest's collar.

"Lucy!" He gave a relieved laugh. "I didn't expect to see you in here! I thought I saw a light—thought maybe someone was breaking in."

She clamped her arms across her chest. Byron had released her now, but she could feel him, the warm, lean strength of him, pressed against her back.

"So," Matt was trying to peer around them into the darkness. "Is there something wrong? Is there—"

"Byron," Byron said quickly. "Byron Wetherly."

The two stared into each other's eyes. Held each other's gazes for an extended moment. Exchanged handshakes, firm and slow.

"Oh, Byron, hello. Matt."

"The new priest," Byron said.

"Well, more of a gofer right now."

Their hands unclasped and slid away.

"Well," Byron said politely. "Welcome to Pine Ridge."

"The necklace," Lucy blurted out. "Do you still have it?"

For a second Matt looked puzzled. Then his grin relaxed.

"Right! That green necklace I found this morning. What happened—did you suddenly remember it was yours?" At Lucy's wan smile, he moved his shoulders in an apologetic shrug. "But . . . I'm so sorry . . . somebody else already came by for it."

Lucy and Byron traded glances. "Who?"

"Well . . . I don't know, actually." Another gesture of apology. "I left it by the altar like I said I would. But I had to leave for a while, and the cleaning lady was here. She said someone came by to claim it."

"But you don't know who it was?" Lucy persisted.

"I sure don't, sorry."

"What about the cleaning lady? Would *she* know who it was?" Byron asked casually.

"Well . . . from what I understand, she knows just about everybody around here. Do you know Mrs. Dempsey?"

"Sure. Come on then, Lucy." Byron nudged her from behind. "We better go."

Nodding, Lucy looked back over her shoulder,

making one last survey of the church. No cold now . . . no fragrance. But her heart was still racing, and her blood still had that chill . . .

"Sorry we worried you," Byron mumbled, pushing past Matt onto the steps.

"I wasn't worried," Matt said.

Lucy glanced up into his face as she passed him. His smile was still warm, still teasing. He gave her a conspiratorial wink, and she quickly glanced away.

As they reached the sidewalk, Matt suddenly called them back.

"Hey, wait a minute—I *do* remember something she said." At Lucy's perplexed look, he added, "The cleaning lady. When the guy came for that necklace."

He was quiet a moment, thinking. Byron's fingers dug sharply into Lucy's shoulder blade.

"Right." Matt nodded. "A guy. That's what she said, a good-looking guy . . . he said he'd gotten it as a present."

"A present?" Lucy echoed. "For what?"

"Not what . . . *who*. For a girl." Matt chuckled. "He said it was a present for a girl he'd met at the Fall Festival."

Lucy froze. A sick taste of fear rose slowly into her throat.

"Did he . . . did he say what her name was?"

Matt cocked his head and thought again. "Just . . . oh, now I remember. Something about New Orleans."

Lucy spun and stared up at Byron.

"Oh my God," she choked. "Angela."

# 29

"Wait—slow down! You're not making any sense."

"Hurry! We've got to get back to the Festival!"

"Lucy, calm *down*! Will you please tell me what's going on—"

"I don't *know* what's going on, okay? Just drive! All I know is that Angela's in some kind of trouble."

"*How* do you know that? And start from the beginning."

Lucy leaned toward him in the front seat, her voice tense with anxiety. "Remember when I told you she was hanging out at the fair with some guy Irene didn't know about? *He* must be the guy who picked up the necklace."

"That's impossible. The necklace doesn't have anything to do with Angela." Byron's hands tightened on the steering wheel. "What *possible* connection could Katherine's stalker have with Angela?"

"I don't know—I don't *know*! But that's why we have to find her!"

"You don't even know if it *is* Angela this guy picked up the necklace for."

"He said New Orleans! And Angela wants to go to New Orleans!"

"So? Lots of people want to go to New Orleans. *I* wouldn't mind going to New Orleans—"

"Call it a hunch then. Just please hurry."

They reached the Festival again in record time. Leaving Byron to follow, Lucy went immediately for the scarecrow-game tent and shoved her way to the front of the line amid irate kids and their equally irate parents. At the entrance she recognized the same girl who'd been there last night, the one with the serious face.

"Where's Angela?" Lucy asked breathlessly.

"Huh! Wouldn't *we* like to know! She left just the two of us here tonight with twice as many brats!"

"But have you seen her?"

"Yeah, a little earlier, but—"

"Please—it's important!"

The girl shrugged. "She said she was going with some guy."

"Going? Going where?"

"I don't know. Getting a ride? Or going away? Or—"

"Was it the same guy she was with last night?"

This time the girl rolled her eyes. "How would I know that? They were pretty busy, if you know what I mean. It's not like I could really see his face."

"Can't you remember anything about him? Anything at all?"

"I think he might have been tall. Maybe dark hair . . . but you know, they were back in the shadows."

As Byron caught up with her, Lucy spun to face him. "We have to go after her."

"After her *where*? How can we go after her if we don't know where she went?"

Lucy looked so desperate that the solemn-faced girl sighed sympathetically, then called out to her coworker. "Did Angela say where she was going tonight?"

"You mean, with that guy?" the other girl called back.

"Yeah."

"Uh . . . something about New Orleans, I think."

"Did they say how? Driving? Flying?"

"Maybe driving. I heard something about a bus."

Again Lucy whirled to face Byron. "We've got to stop her."

As Byron attempted to calm her down, they heard the second girl speak up.

"Oh, hey, wait a minute? Are you Lucy?"

Lucy nodded. "Yes."

"Well, somebody left this for you."

"Was it Angela?"

The girl planted herself in the tent doorway, grabbing some rowdy children, trying to establish some semblance of order. "You know, I'm not really sure, okay? Just somebody left it for you. See? It's got your name on it."

The girl handed her a small manila envelope. Lucy's name was printed across the front, and with trembling fingers, she slid open the flimsy seal across the back.

"It's the necklace," she murmured, her eyes going wide. "I know it is . . . oh, Byron, I can't do this . . . I can't—"

Byron grabbed it away from her and ripped open the flap.

Out fell Angela's car keys.

# 30

He hadn't meant for it to come to this.

At least not with this one . . . and especially not this soon.

He always enjoyed playing with them awhile . . . luring them . . . teasing them . . . manipulating them with praises and with promises . . .

And this one had been so easy, so predictable.

But sometimes, he simply grew tired of them.

Sometimes, after a day or a week or a lifetime, he simply discovered they no longer fit into the well-ordered chaos of his world.

She'd been shocked, of course.

That instant of disbelief—that depth of betrayal in her eyes.

"But don't you remember what you told me?"

she'd pleaded, as he'd tasted the tears of her sorrow. "Don't you remember what you said?"

"Of course," he'd soothed her, "of course I do . . ."

"Don't you remember you promised?"

And he'd pressed her against his heart, and plunged the dagger through her throat, and twisted it with cold, calm ease.

And then he'd smiled.

"Of course I remember, Angela . . . but I lied."

# 31

Lucy stared in disbelief.

As she glanced over at Byron, she saw him hold the envelope upside down and give it a shake. If she hadn't been so stunned, it would have been comical.

"I thought . . ." she stammered, "I really thought—"

"Me, too. But are you sensing anything?"

Trying to break the tension, Lucy bounced the keyless entry in the palm of her hand. "Yeah. I've got a sense these are keys."

"Your psychic abilities are impressive," he deadpanned. He balled up the envelope and tossed it into a trash can, then gave her a curt nod. "Come on."

"Where are we going?" Lucy asked, hurrying to match his long stride.

"You heard her. Let's try the bus depot."

They were there in ten minutes. Not only was the place small, but the waiting room was practically empty. While Byron checked the schedules for southern destinations, Lucy questioned the clerks at the ticket counter. No one remembered Irene Foster's daughter buying a bus ticket today, but after thinking a moment, one of the clerks remembered a young couple bundled in coats and hats and sunglasses who'd taken a southbound express about an hour before.

"I think it's worth a try," Byron decided. "They don't have that much of a head start, and they'll be making stops along the way. It should be easy to catch them."

Lucy felt sick. Sick to her stomach and sick at heart. As she climbed up beside him into the van, she shot him a look of desperation.

"What if you're right?"

"How so?"

"What if this whole thing with the necklace has *nothing* to do with Angela? I mean . . . what if she's really and truly found the love of her life, and they're going off to live happily ever after, and we're going after them and being stupid?"

Byron put the key in the ignition. He stared thoughtfully at the dashboard.

"Then," he said carefully, "at least we know. Then we turn around and come back home. And they have their lives . . . and we have ours."

Lucy sighed. "I can't help it, though. I just still *feel* something—just *here*." She clamped her arms around her midsection and fixed him with a worried frown. "I just feel like something about this isn't right. It's just this awful *nagging* feeling, and it won't go away."

"You're probably feeling a lot of things right now," Byron reminded her. "You thought you had the necklace, and you'd psyched yourself up to face it."

"So did you," she said quietly.

He shrugged. "Emotional roller coaster."

"You're right. I don't know whether to be scared now, or relieved."

"How about a little of both? It's okay, you know, to feel both."

She tried to smile at him, but her emotions were at full pitch. As they sailed along the highway, she leaned against her door and stared out the window of the van. Everything's flowing tonight, she thought vaguely . . . *flowing road . . . flowing van . . . flowing curves . . . flowing hills . . .*

She could still see that strange red moon watching her through the clouds. The color of rust . . . the color of decay. A stain of old dried blood on the wrinkled flesh of the sky.

Shivering, Lucy hunched her shoulders and burrowed deeper into her jacket. It felt like it was getting colder, both outside and in. And the moon . . . that eerie red moon . . . actually seemed to be growing. Growing and glowing among the tops of the trees, like some forgotten Christmas ornament.

Lucy frowned and burrowed deeper. Why did full moons like that make her feel so weird? Make her think of creepy things like . . . like . . .

*Prey . . .*

"What?" She sat up straight and looked at Byron, who looked back at her suspiciously.

"What?" he echoed.

"Did you just say something?"

"Yeah, I said, just pray my brakes hold out."

"Oh my God, don't tell me that—your brakes?"

"Well . . . all these curves sure aren't helping my van."

"Thank you, Byron. That definitely eases my mind, your sharing that with me."

She saw that slow half smile working at one corner of his mouth. She realized that she really loved it when he smiled like that. She wished he'd do it more often.

"Stop staring at me," he said, and, grinning, she turned back to her window.

She closed her eyes. The hum of the motor, the rocking motion of the van on the road . . . she could feel herself drifting off. That pleasant state between sleep and attention, when everything seemed soft and warm and safe. She forced her eyes open and searched for taillights up ahead of them, but the road was so twisted, she couldn't see a thing. There wasn't even traffic out tonight, she suddenly realized. But she could see the slow, pale curls of fog beginning to creep in over the highway . . . blurring the yellow line . . . swallowing the road ahead of them.

*That feeling again.* Gnawing at the pit of her stomach.

"Byron," she said uneasily, "be careful."

He cast her a sidelong glance. "Always."

"No, I mean it. Please."

"Are you okay?"

"Yes . . . just . . . I don't know. Restless. Nervous."

"If you want, we can stop for some coffee the first place we see. It might be a good idea."

She gave a distracted nod. She gazed out into the darkness . . . out at that bloody moon. She wished it would go behind a cloud for the rest of the night . . . she wished it would just go away.

She sensed something beside them on the road.

Something she couldn't actually see, something just out of sight off the shoulder, something moving swiftly through the tall weeds, keeping pace with the van.

*Strange . . .*

Lucy looked over at the speedometer. Sixty. Yet she was sure—she was *certain*—that something was out there running, running even faster than the van could go, running even faster than the wind could go . . .

"Byron," she mumbled.

"What?"

She saw him turn toward her.

Saw his hand slide across the seat and reach for her.

She looked into his eyes . . . deep and black as midnight . . . and in that moment she could see in their depths all the truths and emotions that she'd felt that morning with her hand upon his heart.

A sob went through her.

Byron opened his mouth and started to say her name.

But he never got the chance.

As the dark shape came out of the fog, Byron hit the brakes, the tires screeching, the van skidding, sliding, going into a spin. As they whirled around and around, Lucy could see it there—the huge, black shape silhouetted against the fog, standing on all fours, statuelike in the middle of the road. Watching them . . . *watching them* . . .

She tried to reach for Byron—reached *desperately* for Byron—

But her head slammed the window, and the

van careened off the hill, and all she could think in those last few seconds was *he never got to say it* . . .

*Byron never said my name.*

# 32

*So this is what it's like to die . . .*

Lying there on her back in the grass, all alone in the darkness, she could sense the wet, runny mask of her face—tears? blood?—she couldn't be sure, couldn't be sure she even *had* a face, couldn't be sure about anything except that her body screamed in pain each time she tried to draw even the shallowest of breaths.

*I can't move . . . help . . . somebody, help me . . .*

With a ragged cry, Lucy tried to lift her head, tried to peer through the thick, endless night surrounding her. As in a dream, she could see the faraway sky blazing bright, lit by a giant fire—and along with those sickening smells of pain and fear and despair that threatened to choke her, now there was the gasoline . . . burning rubber . . . white-hot metal . . . and

something else . . . something dear to her
heart . . .

*Byron!*

*That's Byron's van!*

She'd been sitting in the front seat beside
him, and she'd been staring at the moon. That
bloodred moon hovering there behind the trees
and glowing out through the dark, shredded
fabric of the clouds. She'd been staring at the
moon, and then she'd jolted with the first sharp
swerve of the van. Confused and groggy, she'd
heard Byron's shout, the piercing shriek of
brakes and tires; she'd felt the road give way to
air beneath them as they dove off the shoulder
and off the crest of the hill, and out through
the foggy night, plummeting down and down
into nothingness . . .

*Byron? Can you hear me?*

She knew somehow that she hadn't spoken
aloud, knew somehow that her thoughts had
burst free of her pain, only to fall silent among
the shadows. It was so dark out here. So dark,
so frighteningly still, except for those flames
leaping and glowing against the distant
horizon . . .

*Something ran in front us.*

With a moan, Lucy struggled to shut out the pain, struggled to focus her hazy thoughts.

*Byron tried to swerve, he tried to miss hitting it, but something ran in front of us . . .*

She wished she could remember. She wished she could remember what it was that had caused the accident. But there was only the briefest glimmer of memory in that last fatal second, only the briefest image of something caught in headlights as the car veered and left the road.

*What* was *that?*

It seemed so familiar somehow . . .

But her thoughts were fading . . . fading . . . and she knew she was slipping away. In desperation she stared up at the trees overhead, great gnarled branches etched thickly against the black dome of the sky. And then she noticed that moon.

So full and round. So red like blood. Caught in a web of tangled limbs, oozing out through the clouds, wine stains on velvet.

*Byron, I'm so scared! Please help me!*

And that's when she heard it.

The soft rustling sound, like wind sighing through grass. Except that she couldn't *feel* any wind, not even the faintest of breezes, in this heavy night air.

The sound was close by.

Coming even closer . . .

*Oh God!*

Once more she tried to lift herself, to call out for help. But the rustlings were in her head now, in her thoughts and in her pain, like so many urgent whispers, whispers of great importance.

As Lucy's head turned helplessly to one side, she saw shadows all around her, shadows slinking along the ground and through the trees, slivers of black, and pale, pale gray, and sparks of amber light . . .

Terror exploded within her. Even through the paralyzing numbness of pain and shock, she sensed that these were animals, and she sensed why they were here. Instinct told her that she was surrounded, though one stood closer than the others. She could hear the slow, calm rhythm of its breathing as it watched her from a place she couldn't see.

*Oh, God, don't let me die like this!*

She thought of Byron. The vision burst inside her brain with such force that she choked and gagged and vomited blood in the grass. In that one instant of agonizing clarity she saw his midnight eyes, heard his calm, deep voice, telling her not to be afraid. Now she remembered how he'd turned to her in that last split second of his life, his eyes desperate with helplessness and disbelief as he'd reached for her hand. *Did he touch me?* The thought drifted through her mind, light as a feather. *Did we touch one last time?*

But the whispers were louder now, and the fire was brighter than ever, and she was so weak . . . so tired.

*Please . . . please . . . just let me die fast . . .*

Night swayed around her. As tears ran silently down her cheeks, something huge and dark leaned in over her, blocking her view of the sky.

She steeled herself for the end. Felt hot breath caressing her throat . . . smelled the faint, familiar scent of something sweet . . .

*Byron . . . I'm so sorry. . .*

"Byron has gone," the voice murmured. "Only I can save you now."

*Who are you?* What *are you?*

Down . . . down she sank into the endless-ness of time.

And that voice . . . fading far into nothing-ness . . .

"Oh, Lucy . . . There's no name for what we are."